A KNIFE FLASHED IN THE KIOWA'S HAND.

Glidinghawk steeled himself for the bite of the blade, but instead the Kiowa flung it down in front of Glidinghawk. The point stuck in the ground and the hilt quivered with the impact.

His face grim, the Kiowa took another knife from his buckskin pants. "This will be a fair fight."

Glidinghawk looked down at the knife. If he was killed, no one would mourn him. No one would sing the death chants for him.

The mission would be over before it hardly began.

But he could not let the challenge go unanswered—he had too much pride for that.

Slowly, he bent over and plucked the knife from the ground.

POWELL'S ARMY
BY TERENCE DUNCAN

Available wherever paperbacks are sold, or order direct from the Publisher. Send cover price plus 50¢ per copy for mailing and handling to Zebra Books, Dept. 2515, 475 Park Avenue South, New York, N.Y. 10016. Residents of New York, New Jersey and Pennsylvania must include sales tax. DO NOT SEND CASH.

POWELL'S ARMY

#6 RED RIVER DESPERADOES

TERENCE DUNCAN

ZEBRA BOOKS
KENSINGTON PUBLISHING CORP.

ZEBRA BOOKS

are published by

Kensington Publishing Corp.
475 Park Avenue South
New York, NY 10016

First printing: November, 1988

Printed in the United States of America

CHAPTER ONE

Home, Gerald Glidinghawk thought as he gazed at the scattering of teepees around the perimeter of Fort Supply, Indian Territory.

What a goddamned bitter word.

Not his home, of course, but the reservation where he had spent much of his life was similar enough. The resemblance was enough to rouse feelings in him that he tried to keep suppressed most of the time.

The tall, well-knit Omaha Indian strode toward the sutler's store, trying to put the bad memories out of his head. It had been a long time since he had seen his wife and child—too long to be mourning their loss now. They were not dead—not as far as he knew, anyway—but they were as lost to him as if they had been.

Time to put that behind him and concentrate on the job at hand.

"Who the hell's that?" Glidinghawk heard an unshaven corporal asking another soldier as the Omaha walked by them. "Ain't seen him around the fort before."

"Don't know," the corporal's companion replied. "Shoot, the way them redskins come an' go, ain't no

5

way to keep up with them, Kelvin."

The corporal nodded. "Reckon you're right. All the blasted heathens could go somewhere else, as far as I'm concerned. Then maybe white men could make something out of this here Injun Territory."

Glidinghawk stepped up onto the store's porch, unable to shut out the harsh words but attempting to pay as little attention to them as possible. The two soldiers weren't expressing any opinions he hadn't heard plenty of times before.

When he had lived among the white men, there had often been such conversations carried on behind his back. Sometimes the slurs were whispered. Most of the time they were spoken plainly, the speakers caring little that he overhead the insults.

The same thing had been true during his time on the reservation. There he was equally despised for having been raised by a white family. The difference was that on the reservation he had sometimes been forced to fight because of his background. The foolish ones who had pushed him into violence had always regretted it later.

Those days were behind him now. He knew he would not find a home in either world, white or red. The best he could hope for was a family of sorts.

He had found that in Powell's Army, the top-secret undercover unit of civilian investigators who worked for Colonel Amos Powell of the adjutant general's office.

Glidinghawk stepped into the store, inhaling the distinctive mixture of smells that marked such places. Tobacco and coffee and leather and liniment blended together in an aroma that was unmistakable to anyone

6

who had spent much time on the frontier. The place was busy, with several soldiers and a few civilians lined up at the long counter in the rear of the store.

Taking his place at the rear of the line, Glidinghawk waited patiently. He had a few coins in the pocket of his buckskin shirt—damned few, in fact—but enough to buy a pouchful of tobacco for his pipe. As he waited, he became aware that the man in front of him was casting unhappy glances over his shoulder.

The man, a civilian in a brown suit and cream-colored Stetson, frowned narrow-eyed at Glidinghawk for a moment, then looked forward again with a shake of his head. The Omaha heard him mutter, "Disgraceful! These creatures shouldn't be allowed to shop in the same store with white men."

Glidinghawk's mouth tightened, but he made no other response. The young man who was so offended by his presence was slender and well groomed, wearing a neat mustache. There was an air of softness about him suggesting that he had not been in the West for long.

Even though it might be difficult, Glidinghawk was going to ignore him for as long as he possibly could.

The line finally reached the counter, the clerk saying, "Next!" as the young man in the brown suit stepped up.

"I need some tobacco," the young man snapped.

The clerk nodded. "Good thing you got here when you did then, mister. We're just about out. I got one pouch left, but that's all."

The young man frowned and said, "One pouch? That's all? When will you have more?"

"Oh, there should be some coming in with our next

7

shipment of supplies," the clerk answered with a shrug. "That'll be day after tomorrow. Reckon you can make this last that long?" He reached under the counter and lifted a pouch of tobacco into view.

"I guess I'll have to," the young man grumbled.

Glidinghawk had been listening to the conversation with interest. Now he leaned slightly to one side and spoke around the man in front of him. "I wanted some tobacco, too," he said. "Why don't you split what's in the pouch and sell it to both of us?"

Before the clerk could respond, the young man jerked his head around and said, "No! I'll not share anything with the likes of you." He slapped some coins down on the counter. "There! The transaction is completed. Now out of my way, Indian."

Glidinghawk stayed where he was, slightly crowding the man against the counter. "That was rather rude of you, my friend," he grated, his university education easy to hear in his voice, even through his annoyance.

"I don't give a damn. I told you to move."

Glidinghawk locked eyes with the young man. There was a matching stubbornness in their features as they glared at each other. The musty air in the store suddenly took on a feeling of impending violence.

"Look here," the clerk said hastily, bending forward over the counter. "This fella has already paid me for the tobacco, Injun. Ain't nothing either one of us can do about it. Why don't you just mosey on? Nobody wants trouble."

Glidinghawk ignored the clerk. To the young man, he said, "You could sell me some of the tobacco in that pouch yourself. I'll pay you more than it's worth."

The man smiled nastily. "I never saw an Indian with

8

enough money to buy anything. All any of you want is handouts from the government. You'll not get any such from me."

Glidinghawk tensed, his throat tight and hot, the urge to smash the young man's smirking face strong within him. But a hard grip on his arm from behind made him change his mind.

"Forget it, redskin," a voice growled. "You're lookin' at a lot more trouble than you know."

Glidinghawk glanced behind him and saw a burly noncom holding him. There were sergeant's stripes on the sleeves of the blue tunic that was stretched tight across brawny shoulders.

"I don't like being talked to the way this man is doing," Glidinghawk said, realizing the futility of his words even as he spoke them. This sergeant wasn't going to take his side in the dispute, and he knew it.

"Don't matter," the soldier said. "This is the new Indian agent, mister. I reckon he can talk to you any way he likes."

Glidinghawk's eyes narrowed to slits. He turned his head for a moment and regarded the self-satisfied smile on the young man's face.

The sergeant went on, "I'm just tryin' to keep you out of trouble, redskin. Take my advice and get out of here."

Glidinghawk took a deep breath. "I suppose you're right." With a shake of his head, he started toward the door of the store. Behind him, Fort Supply's new Indian agent tossed the pouch of tobacco up in the air and then caught it lightly. Glidinghawk could feel the man's arrogant gaze following him.

He stepped out onto the porch, inhaled deeply

again.

There would be a chance later to settle the score with the brash young civilian.

The clatter of stagecoach wheels drew Glidinghawk's attention. He looked again at the sprawling Indian settlement outside the fort. The road cut through it, and along the dusty ruts rolled one of the durable Concord coaches. Even though this was Indian Territory and supposedly unsettled by white men, that was a charade for the most part. Between the soldiers and the army's civilian employees and the ranchers who leased land from the Indians, there were plenty of whites in the Territory. Several stage lines crisscrossed its terrain. This road came into Fort Supply from the north and then continued on south, toward the Red River and Texas.

The stage raised a considerable cloud of dust as it came to a stop in front of the store, which doubled as a stage station. Glidinghawk blinked and moved to the other end of the porch, away from the worst of the eye-stinging stuff. As the breeze shredded the cloud and blew it away, the driver turned around on the box and called to his passengers, "Fort Supply, folks. We'll only be here long enough to change hosses, so don't wander off."

Glidinghawk leaned on the railing at the end of the porch and watched as half a dozen passengers alighted from the coach to stretch their legs. Four of them were obviously drummers of some kind, florid, fleshy-faced men in loud suits. The other two passengers were the ones who drew Glidinghawk's attention.

There was something about the tall, lean man who hopped lithely from the stage that said he was a Texan.

From his boots to his dark, flat-crowned hat, he bore the look of a man who was at home on the frontier.

Maybe it was the casualness of the way he wore the big .44 belted around his hips. The pistol's walnut grips were worn smooth with use.

The Texan turned and lifted a hand to assist the final passenger off the stage. As a woman's arm emerged from the shadows of the coach, her fingers taking the Texan's hand, interest quickened in the soldiers who were idly watching. Except for squaws, the sight of women was an unusual one around these parts.

And there was a good chance that Fort Supply had never seen a woman as lovely as the one who stepped off the stage now.

She had thick, lustrous red hair underneath the neat turquoise hat perched on her head. Her stylish traveling outfit was the same shade, and the frilly white blouse she wore under the jacket was cut daringly low, revealing the swell of high, full breasts. As she took the arm of the Texan, he made some low-voiced comment to her that provoked a peal of merry laughter.

The woman glanced around as she and the tall man started up the steps onto the store's porch. She was obviously well aware of the admiring stares she was receiving—and she was not disturbed by them either. As a lady of dubious reputation—which she plainly was—only a few rungs above the station of a soiled dove, she had to be used to the lustful stares of men.

Glidinghawk looked at her, too, letting his eyes rove over the rich curves of her body. As the couple went across the porch, the young Indian agent stepped out the door and moved aside to let them enter. The young

11

man nodded to the lady and touched the brim of his hat.

Then, as he glanced up, he saw the Omaha Indian standing at the end of the porch, watching the redhead with open lust in his eyes.

The Indian agent's mouth twitched angrily. He strode down the porch toward Glidinghawk. "I thought I told you to get back to your teepee, Indian," he barked as he came to a stop in front of the Omaha.

"I'm going," Glidinghawk replied in a surly voice. "What's wrong with watching the stage come in first?"

"What's wrong is the way you were staring at that white lady, you savage! You Indians are going to continue to have trouble. I'm charged with looking out for your interests, so you heed what I'm saying to you."

"Thank you so much," Glidinghawk said acidly. "So kind of the Great White Father to send a man like you to help us."

The agent flushed angrily. After a moment, he visibly controlled his emotions and said, "There's nothing worse than a savage with a little education."

"Unless it's a white man with even less," Glidinghawk shot back.

The noncom who had interceded inside the store had lounged out onto the porch after the Indian agent, and now he came toward the angry pair. "Here, Injun!" he said sharply. "I told you to get out of here and stop causin' trouble."

"I can handle this, Sergeant Foster," the Indian agent snapped. "The sooner these people learn who is in command here, the better things will be."

"I know, sir," the sergeant said smoothly. "But some of them are just too hardheaded to deal with properly.

12

You let me have a talk with this one, sir, and I'll teach him some manners."

Glidinghawk stiffened at the threat. The Indian agent nodded slowly. "Probably a good idea, Sergeant," he said. "I'll leave him to you." Without a backward look, the slender young man stalked off, stepping down off the porch and heading for the fort's headquarters building.

As the noncom turned toward Glidinghawk, the Omaha said in a low voice, "I don't intend to be manhandled, Sergeant. Not without fighting back."

"That's a good way for an Indian to get hung," the sergeant told him. "But relax, mister. I'm not just about to get into a scrape because some pompous ass got his nose out of joint."

Glidinghawk frowned in surprise. "I see we agree on the new Indian agent."

"Damn right." The sergeant gave him a thoughtful stare for a moment, then said, "Just keep out of his way and don't cause trouble around here, mister, or I really will have to put you down."

Glidinghawk nodded. "I'll keep that in mind."

"You do that." The sergeant turned and walked away.

Glidinghawk raised a leg and agilely stepped over the railing around the porch, dropping to the dirt at the side of the building. He walked toward the rear of the store. The sutler had quarters back there, and there was an outhouse behind the building, well away from it, as was the custom. Glidinghawk glanced around, saw no one watching, and headed for the little two-holer.

He had been inside the flimsy structure for about

13

two minutes when the door opened. The tall Texan from the stagecoach stepped in, his nose wrinkling in distaste. He said to the Omaha, who was leaning against the wall, "We've had meetings in some mighty strange places, but damned if this ain't the worst one yet."

Gerald Glidinghawk grinned at Landrum Davis, one of his partners in Powell's Army, and said, "I agree, so let's get it over with. What the hell are we doing in Indian Territory?"

CHAPTER TWO

"How much do you know already?" Landrum asked, still grimacing at the smell in the little shack.

"Not much," Glidinghawk replied. "Powell's telegram told me to come here and wait until you and Celia showed up. He said Fox would already be here and for me to follow his lead." The Omaha chuckled. "That part of it worried me, but it was no trouble. Preston was acting the way he usually does. It was easy enough to argue with him, since that's what he seemed to want."

Landrum echoed Glidinghawk's chuckle. He slipped a leather wallet out of his jacket and removed a folded piece of paper from it. "The dispatch from Amos should explain things," he said. "At least you'll know as much as I do."

Glidinghawk took the paper and smoothed it out, reading the words on it in the dim light coming through the traditional half-moon cutout in the shed's door.

To A, B, C, and D
From AP

One of the army's missions is to curtail the illicit whiskey trade. Whiskey is prohibited in unsettled territories, Indian reservations etc. A recent drive to curb the trade in Indian Territory only resulted in the traders establishing themselves in safety somewhere south of the Red River, possibly in what settlers call the Copper Brakes. The terrain is so vast and rugged that not even intensive army patrolling curbs these whiskey runs. It is a lucrative business; the traders offer small amounts of rotgut whiskey in return for money which the Indians obtain by raiding, robbing, and stealing from the settlers in north Texas. In addition, there are rumors that the whiskey runners trade for squaws, who are treated as chattel.

The business is largely run by rough desperadoes, well versed in knife and gun. They have spies at Fort Supply and the army suspects that some crooked Indian agents are involved.

Because of Agent D's familiarity with bureaucracy, he will be sent out to the Indian Nations as an Indian agent attached to Fort Supply. It is suggested that Agent B pose as an outcast of his tribe hostile to both reservation Indians and to white society. As a thoroughly immoral outcast, he should be able to infiltrate the band of traders working within the Nations. Agents A and C will attempt to track down the source of the illicit whiskey production, believed to take place at a headquarters in north Texas.

Glidinghawk looked up from the dispatch sent by Amos Powell and considered the colonel's orders. He smiled slightly, but his eyes were bleak as he said, "This part about being an outcast should be simple to carry off. The reservation Indians and white society are both hostile enough to me."

"You can see why Fox was trying to pick a fight with you," Landrum said. "We don't know who the whiskey traders are working with here at Fort Supply, though, so you might make this feud with the Fox last a while. Let plenty of people see how you don't get along with the new Indian agent."

Glidinghawk nodded. "I had a hunch it must be something like that. I'm beginning to have an idea of how Colonel Powell's mind works."

As was only to be expected, he thought. The four-member team known in certain high-level military circles as Powell's Army had been together for a couple of years now, their missions taking them across the West from Arizona to Montana Territory. Their last assignment, several months earlier, had seen them unraveling a web of corruption in a government commission headquartered in Denver. Since that time, the group had lain low, each one going his separate way until they were needed again.

And now they were needed, obviously.

Glidinghawk had not been surprised to see former First Lieutenant Preston Kirkwood Fox masquerading as an Indian agent. It was the type of cover identity which the young man could maintain fairly easily. Originally the team's liaison officer, Fox had been forced to go undercover after a disastrous mission in Dodge City. He still harbored hopes of someday being returned to active duty, Glidinghawk knew, but for the time being, Fox was at least trying to fit in as a member of the team. So far, his efforts had met with mixed results.

Landrum Davis, former Confederate soldier, former Texas Ranger, was the nominal leader of the group, simply because he was the oldest and most experienced in the ways of the frontier. He and Glidinghawk got along well most of the time, and the Omaha had to admit that Landrum was the closest thing he had to a friend now.

The final member of the group had disembarked from the stage a little earlier with Landrum. Celia Louise Burnett was the daughter of an army officer who had been killed in an Indian raid, along with Celia's mother. Celia had grown up in a succession of forts and been educated back East in an exclusive finishing school. All of them worried about Celia, from Colonel Powell on down. But the beautiful young red-head had proven to be a capable agent, even though she was a bit quick to give in to the temptations of life's wilder side. Glidinghawk admired her, as he did Landrum Davis. The jury was still out on Preston Fox, but Glidinghawk was willing to give him the benefit of the doubt most of the time.

Glidinghawk handed the dispatch back to Landrum, who stored it away again. "Where are you and Celia headed?"

"Truscott, Texas," Landrum replied. "Not much of a town, but Amos thinks the whiskey traders are probably cooking the stuff between there and the Red River. We're going to try to root them out if they are."

Glidinghawk nodded. "Not an easy job. That's rough country there, south of the Red."

Landrum shrugged. "We've got it to do. The hard job seems to be yours this time around, no matter what you say. Those whiskey runners find out you're working for the army, they'll cut your throat right quick — if you're lucky."

The Omaha grimaced. "I'll manage. If something goes wrong . . . well, it won't be any great loss."

Glidinghawk started for the door, but Landrum reached out to stop him with a firm grip on his arm. With a frown of concern on his face, the Texan said, "What's wrong, Gerald? You look as grim as I've seen you lately."

Glidinghawk shook his head, unsure how to answer Landrum's question. He wasn't sure he even knew himself what was bothering him.

No, that wasn't true. He did know. But would Landrum — would any white man — truly understand?

"I look out from this fort and I see people who were once my own," Glidinghawk said slowly. "I may have never lived with these tribes, but I know them. And I see how far they have fallen. They beg for food and shelter now, and that is all they know."

"You're talking about the ones who choose to live around the forts," Landrum pointed out. "There are still plenty out here in the Nations who are doing well for themselves. The ones over east of here they call the Civilized Tribes. They've got laws and governments of their own. The Cheyenne and the Arapaho and the others in this part of the Territory, well, a lot of them are still out there living like they used to."

"Yes. Indeed they are. Raiding and stealing and making sure that eventually the white man will have no choice but to wipe them out. It's a war the Indians can't win, Landrum. All they can do is fight to the end."

Landrum Davis shook his head. "I don't know what

19

to tell you, Gerald. The world may not be the way we'd want it to be, but we got to do the best we can with the hand we're dealt."

Glidinghawk nodded curtly. "Don't worry about me, Landrum. I'll do my job."

"I know you will." Landrum wrinkled his nose again. "Now let's get the hell out of here. That coach will be pulling out soon. If you need to get in touch with us, you'll probably have to go through Fox."

Glidinghawk inclined his head in understanding.

Landrum went first, calling back softly to Glidinghawk that no one was around. The Omaha slipped out, too, and slouched up to the street in front of the sutler's. He paused long enough to see Landrum and Celia climbing aboard the stagecoach once again. Neither of them even glanced in his direction, which was the way it was supposed to be.

He wondered when he would see them again.

Or if he would see them again. This job was going to be dangerous, as all their assignments were. The men who trafficked in illegal whiskey wouldn't hesitate to kill anyone who interfered with their plans.

The jehu climbed on to the stage, cracked his whip, and yelled hoarsely at his new team. The animals strained against the lines, and the stage lurched into motion.

Glidinghawk stood beside the building and watched until it was dwindled into the distance, finally becoming a small black dot that disappeared into the haze of dust.

Preston Kirkwood Fox was still angry as he waited

in the small anteroom outside the office of Fort Supply's commanding officer. Glidinghawk had certainly been obnoxious. Fox had counted on that reaction from the Omaha when he began his disparaging remarks in the sutler's store. Glidinghawk was intelligent, Fox had to give him that much. He had picked up on the ruse immediately.

But he had seemed to put a little more feeling than was necessary into his act.

That was typical of Glidinghawk, though, Fox thought. Despite his background in the white man's world, Glidinghawk's soul was that of a red man. Brooding hostility came naturally to him.

The corporal who served as the commanding officer's clerk said, "You can go in now." There was a decided lack of respect in the man's voice that rankled Fox.

The corporal had no way of knowing that the man he was talking to was still an officer at heart. To him Fox was just another bureaucrat from Washington, someone to be tolerated but not admired.

Carrying himself militarily erect, Fox stepped into the colonel's office. Laurence Selmon was a career officer, short and thick bodied with graying rust colored hair. He had a habit of chewing his thick mustache, as he was now as he studied the paperwork spread out on his desk.

"What can I do for you, Follet?" he asked without looking up.

Fox waited for an invitation to sit down in the visitor's chair in front of the desk, but none was forthcoming. Standing there awkwardly, he suppressed his anger at the way he had been treated here at Fort

Supply.

The officers and men here knew him only as Preston Follet, a young Indian agent on his first assignment for the Bureau of Indian Affairs.

"I just had a run-in with one of the bucks here at the fort," Fox said. "An Omaha from the looks of him."

"What happened?" Selmon asked, showing a little more interest now.

"The savage threatened me," Fox declared. That was stretching the truth some. "All I did was state my opinion that Indians should not shop at the same stores as white men, and the lout took offense."

Selmon heaved a sigh. "Did the brave attack you?"

"If he had he would have regretted it," Fox said confidently. "No. One of your men happened to be there and he stepped in to put a stop to it before things went too far. Sergeant Foster, I believe it was."

Fox knew quite well the noncommissioned supply officer had been Bradley Foster. He had studied the duty roster of the troops assigned before even arriving at the fort. Preparation was an important part of the job. He had never been able to get that through to Landrum and the others, who sometimes went off on the wildest tangents.

Then, remembering some of the things he himself had done in Montana and the Colorado Territories, Fox abandoned that line of thought for the moment.

Colonel Selmon was nodding. "Foster is a good man," he said. "I'm glad things did not get worse."

"The sergeant offered to have a talk with the Indian and straighten him out. I hope he won't cause any more trouble."

Selmon shook his head and said, "Foster's got

enough sense not to kill the buck. He'll just rough him up a bit, teach him a lesson." The colonel squinted shrewdly at Fox and went on, "That doesn't bother you, one of my men getting tough with an Indian?"

"Why should it?" Fox asked.

"It is your job to look out for the savages," Selmon pointed out.

"That doesn't mean I have to adore the bloody heathens. No, Colonel, I'm an administrator. I try to make things run smoothly. That doesn't mean I have to coddle the Indians." Fox sniffed. "I think we treat them rather well, considering the way they've held up the nation's rightful expansion across the West."

Selmon leaned back in his chair and chuckled. "That's a lot more practical attitude than we've seen from some of the do-gooders and sky pilots who come out here to help the so-called noble red men."

Fox smiled thinly. "I'm a practical man."

"And an ambitious one, I'd wager. You know how to get ahead in life, don't you, Follet?" It was a statement, not a question.

"I like to think so," Fox answered smugly.

"I'll keep that in mind," Selmon said with a sage nod. "It's hard enough for civilians and the military to get along. A good attitude makes it a lot easier." Briskly, the colonel straightened some of his papers. "Now, is that why you came to see me, Follet—to tell me about your problem with that brave?"

"Well, you are the commanding officer of the fort, Colonel. I felt you should know about it."

"Do you know the Indian's name?"

Fox shook his head. "No, but like I said, I think he's an Omaha. And he's new here. I saw him riding in on one of those crowbait ponies earlier today."

"I'll talk to Foster," Selmon decided, "tell him to keep an eye on the buck. We don't want any troublemakers around here."

Fox felt a surge of satisfaction. "Very good. Thank you, sir." Without thinking, he almost came to attention and saluted, catching himself just in time to stop the gesture.

He said his farewells and left the office, pleased with himself. He had planted the idea with Selmon that he was an ambitious sort, willing to do whatever it took to get what he wanted—even cooperating with illegal whiskey traders.

He had no reason to suspect that the colonel was part of the ring . . . but Selmon might be involved. Fox would wait and see if someone approached him with a shady deal.

And he had established Glidinghawk as a troublemaker. That could help the Omaha accomplish his mission.

Or get him killed.

CHAPTER THREE

Glidinghawk knew there were some things that could not be rushed. He avoided Fox for the next couple of days, not wanting to overdo his pose as an angry outcast. It seemed certain from Amos Powell's dispatch that the whiskey runners had confederates here at Fort Supply, but there was no way of knowing who they were.

They would have to come to him — and he would have to be ready.

There was not much to do around the post. Glidinghawk found a spot behind the mess hall where he could roll his blankets at night. During the day he sat in the shade, a sullen look on his face, and watched the activity at the fort. Some of the soldiers cast suspicious glances at him, as if they thought he might be a spy for a band of renegades, but Glidinghawk ignored them.

The Indians themselves were cool toward him. The few times he spoke to any of them, they answered his questions curtly and then moved on, obviously having heard that he had been raised by a white family and educated back East. It was plain that they despised him.

Blanket Indians, Glidinghawk thought. They've given up their way of life to settle for white men's leavings, yet they look down on me.

Pride was a powerful thing. And that was about all some of these Indians had left.

He was half dozing, his back leaned up against the trunk of a small tree, when he heard an angry snort. Glidinghawk glanced up through slitted eyes and saw a Kiowa brave standing over him, arms folded, face set in lines of disgust.

"White man's dog!" the Kiowa snapped.

Glidinghawk stayed where he was, but something about his indolent pose changed, became somehow more alert. "You speak to me?" he said.

"I see no other white man's dog around here," the Kiowa replied haughtily. "I look around and I see warriors. I see my people. There is only one I see who has no soul."

Glidinghawk's mouth curved in a humorless smile. "I see you've heard of me."

The Kiowa made a hawking sound in his throat and spat, the gob of spittle landing close to Glidinghawk's outstretched foot. Several drops splattered on to his moccasin. Having expressed himself, the Kiowa turned on his heel and began to stalk away.

Glidinghawk closed his eyes for a second and took a deep breath, suppressing the true anger he felt and considering the situation in light of the mission he was on. This was just the sort of opportunity he needed. There were plenty of people around, some of whom had probably heard the Kiowa's insulting words.

Then he let the genuine anger flow back into him, using it to propel him as he came to his feet and

26

launched himself into a dive at the Kiowa.

Glidinghawk slammed into the man, tackling him around the waist. Both of them fell, sprawling heavily to the ground. The Kiowa let out a howl of rage and twisted around, driving an elbow at Glidinghawk's face. Glidinghawk jerked his head to the side so that the blow missed, then rolled and came lithely up on his feet.

"I am no man's dog!" he told the other man. "There is only one cur here, Kiowa!"

The warrior came up off the ground with a snarl, throwing himself with outstretched arms at Glidinghawk. Glidinghawk slapped the reaching hands aside and darted out of the way. The Kiowa took a couple of stumbling steps before he could catch his balance and right himself.

Glidinghawk's laugh rang across the parade ground of the fort. "You've been too long away from the battle," he mocked. "You fight like a woman."

The Kiowa shook his head and growled. His hand groped at his waist, and Glidinghawk realized the man was reaching for a weapon that was no longer there. The knife or tomahawk he had carried was now gone, traded for the security of an existence on the fringes of the white man's world.

"I will kill you," the Kiowa grated. "I will tear your miserable white man's heart out!"

"I'm waiting," Glidinghawk said calmly.

The man lunged forward again, and this time Glidinghawk didn't quite get out of his way. The Kiowa had moved a little faster than he had expected. His fingers grasped Glidinghawk's buckskin shirt and yanked, throwing the Omaha off balance. The Kiowa's

27

hard fist thudded into Glidinghawk's belly, knocking the air out of his lungs.

Glidinghawk blocked the Kiowa's next blow, letting the man's fist slide along his left arm until he could pivot and trap the man's wrist in a viselike grip. Glidinghawk bent at the waist, using the Kiowa's own strength and momentum against him, tossing the warrior right over his back. The Kiowa smashed into the hard ground and let out a groan, but before it was hardly past his lips, Glidinghawk was on him, wrestling with him. They rolled about, raising a cloud of dust, each man striving desperately for the hold that would give him victory.

Vaguely, Glidinghawk heard the whoops and cries of the crowd that had gathered around them. Indians of many different tribes scurried up to watch the fight. A few years earlier, these warriors had been allies and enemies, depending on which band they rode with.

Now they were spectators.

Glidinghawk began to wonder if he had misjudged the Kiowa. The man was strong and wiry and fought with a consuming anger. He had obviously not been a reservation Indian for very long.

After several minutes of wrestling around in the dirt, however, Glidinghawk found himself with a secure hold around the Kiowa's neck. He had his arms under the Kiowa's arms, the hands locked at the back of the other man's neck. Enough pressure in this hold would crack the Kiowa's spine.

Glidinghawk didn't want to kill him. Holding tightly enough to keep his opponent immobilized, Glidinghawk climbed to his feet, bring the Kiowa with him. "Call me a dog, will you?" Glidinghawk said through

28

gritted teeth, aware of the silence that fallen over the ring of onlookers. They sensed that at any moment they could be witnessing a man's death.

"Hold on there!" a harsh voice called. The circle of Indians around Glidinghawk and the Kiowa began to part rapidly.

Glidinghawk hesitated, his face still contorted in fury. He glanced over and saw the burly, blue-uniformed figure striding through the crowd. It was the same sergeant who had stepped in during the encounter with Fox. Foster, that was his name, Glidinghawk remembered. A supply sergeant.

Foster stopped in front of Glidinghawk and the Kiowa and put his hands on his hips. He shook his head and said, "I see you just can't seem to get along with folks, mister."

Glidinghawk increased the pressure on his captive's neck, canting his head forward. The Kiowa made a strangled sound of pain low in his throat. "He insulted me," Glidinghawk said to Foster.

The sergeant's right hand moved, coming up with the service revolver from his holster. His speed was surprising in a man so big. Drawing the hammer of the Colt back to full cock, he lined the barrel on Glidinghawk's forehead and said, "I don't care how much of a son of a bitch he is, let him go."

Foster's voice was flat and cold, and Glidinghawk could see the menace in his eyes. The noncom wouldn't hesitate to shoot him, and given the current state of affairs in Indian Territory, he probably wouldn't come in for much trouble from his superiors for the killing.

Glidinghawk waited for a moment, pushing the situation as far as he could. Then he unlaced his fingers and released the Kiowa, shoving him away with a grunt and an arrogant sneer.

"I do not kill women," he said curtly, "and this one is little better."

The Kiowa cast another hate-filled glance at him, then walked away unsteadily, rubbing his aching neck. The crowd began to disperse, realizing that the momentary respite from boredom was over.

Foster uncocked his gun and slid it back into its holster, snapping the flap down over it. "I'm glad you came to your senses," he said to Glidinghawk. "I hate to kill a man on as pretty a day as this."

Glidinghawk grunted and started to turn away.

Foster reached out to stop him. Holding Glidinghawk's arm with sausagelike fingers, he said, "You're one tough bastard, aren't you?"

Glidinghawk shrugged out of the sergeant's grip. "I wish only to be treated fairly. To be left alone."

"The world ain't going to treat nobody fair," Foster said with a shake of his head. "You want something, Indian, you've got to reach out and take it. I'll bet there's things you want, ain't there?"

Grudgingly, Glidinghawk replied, "I want many things. But I have learned to live without them."

Foster jerked a thumb toward the scattering of teepees and lodges. "Eats at a man like you to see this, don't it? You miss the old days."

"All I really know of the times before this is what I have heard the old men speak of." The Omaha's words took on an increasingly bitter tone as he went on, "The Kiowa said I have no soul. Perhaps he was right. I know I have no home."

Foster clapped a hand on Glidinghawk's shoulder. Glidinghawk did not move, although the touch made him want to flinch away. "Hell, could be worse," Foster said. "We could all be dead somewheres. At least as long as we're alive, things might get better."

"Maybe," Glidinghawk said noncommittally.

Foster nodded and then admonished sternly, "Now you stay out of trouble, fella. Next time could be a lot worse."

Glidinghawk stared at him without making any reply. After a moment, Foster turned and walked away.

Glidinghawk looked around, saw that he was being ignored again now, by soldiers and Indians alike.

Once more—always—he was alone in the crowd.

Supply Sergeant Bradley Foster shrugged his shoulders, trying to pull a little more warmth out of the uniform jacket he wore. Summer was still a ways off, and the nights were downright cold here on the High Plains. Stars burned brilliantly overhead, and he could see their twinkling reflections on the surface of the nearby Canadian River.

He had ridden out from Fort Supply after evening mess. No one paid much attention to his comings and goings. Things were fairly relaxed at the fort right now. The savages were behaving themselves in Indian Territory.

Of course, they were also crossing the Red River regularly into Texas to carry out their depredations, but that worry belonged to the Rangers and the troops stationed in the Lone Star State.

And without those raids, Foster thought, the redskins wouldn't have the loot they needed to buy whiskey. He and his partners wouldn't like that at all.

Foster pulled a flask out of his pocket and took a quick nip. Maybe that would warm him up. As he licked his lips, he muttered aloud, "Dammit, Arlie, where are you?"

The meeting had been scheduled to take place at least a half hour earlier, but Arlie Moody hadn't shown up yet. That was like Arlie. He had probably gotten busy swilling rotgut or bedding some fat, greasy squaw and forgotten all about where he was supposed to be.

Foster heard the quiet sound of horses approaching. He tensed in the saddle. The newcomers were probably Moody and some of his brothers, but it didn't pay to take chances. His hand went to the already unsnapped flap of his holster and rested on the butt of his pistol.

Three shapes appeared out of the shadows. In the darkness, their forms seemed at first monstrous and misshapen, but then they resolved themselves into three men on horseback. The burly noncom relaxed as a familiar voice called out softly, "Foster? That you?"

"Over here, Arlie," Foster replied.

Arlie Moody rode up to Foster's side, followed closely by the other two horsemen. Moody jerked his head toward them and said, "I brung Dirk and Ebenezer with me. That all right?"

Foster nodded. "Sure. Howdy, boys."

The two youngest Moody brothers grunted. That was the extent of their greeting. Like the rest of the clan, they were a sullen and surly pair. Talking to any of the Moody family was sort of like poking a possum with a stick, Foster thought. You never knew what they were going to do.

"We'll be ready for another run in about a week," Arlie Moody said. "When you reckon would be a good time to come?"

"There are no patrols scheduled for next Thursday and Friday," Foster replied. "Might be some last-minute changes, but it ain't likely. Nobody'll bother you."

"Better not, or there'll be shootin'," Arlie promised in his gravelly voice. The Texan was tall and broad-shouldered, bulky in a buffalo coat. Foster had seen him in the daylight plenty of times, and Arlie Moody was not a very impressive specimen. Perpetually unshaven, his clothes old and crudely patched, his black Stetson battered, Arlie looked like the hardcase he was.

But he was plenty tough and ruthless, and Foster could admire him for that. The other four Moody brothers were every bit as rugged as Arlie, but he had a certain spark of cunning that they lacked.

"You had any luck findin' somebody to help me out up here?" Arlie asked. "You know I got to leave some o' the boys home to pertect Ma and the still. Makes it hard to deliver the stuff once I'm over the line with it."

Foster nodded. "I've got my eye on somebody. He might work out real well for us. He's tough, and he's got no love for either the army or the Indians."

"What's his name?"

Chuckling, Foster replied, "Listen to this — he's called Gerald Glidinghawk."

Arlie sat up straight in the saddle, and one of the other brothers — Ebenezer, Foster thought it was — exclaimed, "A goddamn Injun? What the hell's wrong with you, Foster?"

Arlie turned on him, lifting an arm and whipping it around. His calloused hand cracked across the face of the boy who had spoken.

"Shut your damn mouth!" Arlie growled. "I do the talking for this family." He looked back at Foster. "You trust an Injun, Foster?"

"I don't trust anybody," Foster said bluntly. "Not even you, Arlie. But this Omaha is an interesting character. Raised in a white family, had some schoolin' back East. The other Indians hate him, and he don't like them much better. And of course, the whites don't have any use for him." The sergeant grinned. "But maybe we do."

Arlie still sounded dubious as he replied, "You be sure you're right about this, Foster. We'll be seein' you next week. Maybe you can bring this Glidinghawk buck along."

"We'll see," Foster nodded. He watched the whiskey runners ride away into the night.

He could almost smell the money they were all going to make before this was over.

CHAPTER FOUR

Truscott, Texas, wasn't much to look at, Landrum thought as he peered through the window of the stagecoach. One dusty main street lined with businesses, a few crossroads with residences on them. But it was a growing community, as was evidenced by the impressive brick structure on one corner. It was the biggest building in town, and a sign over its entrance proclaimed it to be the First Bank of Truscott.

And the only bank of Truscott, Landrum mused wryly.

He had been here before, had in fact spent quite a bit of time in Texas just before the mission that had taken Powell's Army to Dodge City. There was a good chance that some of the folks in town would remember him.

He glanced at Celia, sitting beside him on the hard bench seat of the coach. The citizens of Truscott wouldn't remember Celia. She had never set foot here before. Landrum was willing to bet that she would make an impression on the good people of Truscott, though.

Ever since starting this journey, Celia had been forced to fend off the advances of the men traveling

35

with them. She was adept at that, and a few hard glances from Landrum had helped discourage the lustful drummers. Sure they took her for a loose woman — they were supposed to. But that didn't mean she had to sit there and let herself be pawed by every horny salesman in the West.

Celia sighed as the stagecoach came to a stop in front of Truscott's way station. Landrum smiled thinly and asked, "Glad to be here?"

"Of course, darling," she answered.

The endearment was for the benefit of their fellow passengers, Landrum thought. Right now Celia probably wasn't too happy with him, or with Amos Powell for that matter. She was the type of young woman who liked bright lights, good whiskey, laughter, and the faint whispering slap of cards being dealt.

This little settlement in the wilds of north Texas had nothing to offer her.

But Truscott was close to the area known as the Copper Brakes, and according to Amos, that was where the whiskey runners were thought to have their headquarters. It was up to Landrum and Celia to locate them and put them out of business — without getting killed in the process.

As usual, the drummers left the stage first. Landrum waited for them to disembark, then stepped down and offered his arm to Celia. She took it, coughing delicately as she moved out of the coach. Her gloved hands brushed dust from her traveling outfit.

As she and Landrum started into the station, one of the hostlers spotted the tall Texan and exclaimed, "Why, howdy, Mr. Davis! Didn't expect to see you back."

"I never expected to come back to this damned place," Landrum growled, his voice none too friendly.

The young hostler frowned in surprise. He remembered that Landrum Davis could be fairly sullen when he had been drinking, but overall he had seemed like a friendly-enough fellow during his previous visit to Truscott. With a shrug, the man went about this work. Folks had a right to change, he supposed.

Landrum and Celia went into the building. Landrum saw the stationmaster puttering around behind his ticket window. He went over to the man and said, "Remember me, Erle?"

The balding, middle-aged stationmaster looked up, nodded when he saw who had spoken. "Why, sure, Mr. Davis," he said. "I recollect you bein' here last year, wasn't it? What can I do for you?"

"My . . . wife . . . and I are looking for a place to stay," Landrum said. "Any places in town for rent?"

He put just enough emphasis on the word *wife* to make it plain that Celia wasn't any such thing.

Celia stepped up closer to Landrum and put her hand on his arm. In a low voice that was still audible to the stationmaster, she said, "Are you sure we have to stay in this awful place, Landrum? Can't we go on down to Fort Worth?"

"Not until we make some more money," Landrum hissed. He turned his attention back to the stationmaster and snapped, "Well? What about it?"

The man nodded. "I think the old Stanley place is for rent. Harv Stanley died a few months ago, and his missus went to live with her sister down in Knox City. You could go talk to Mr. Watts over at the bank. He's handlin' Miz Stanley's affairs."

"Thanks," Landrum said. He turned and walked out of the station, Celia having to hurry slightly to keep up with his long-legged stride. They angled across the street toward the new bank.

Randolph Watts was the president of the First Bank of Truscott, and he was more than happy to sit down with Landrum and Celia and discuss their renting the vacant Stanley house.

"It's just been sitting there since Harv passed on," Watts said from behind the desk in his narrow office. He was a beefy man in his fifties. "There's probably a few things that will need a little fixing up."

"That's no problem," Landrum said.

"As long as the place is nice," Celia added.

"Well, it's plain," Watts said. "Don't know if a lady like you would consider it nice or not, ma'am. But it's got a good sound roof. It'll keep out the spring thunderstorms."

Landrum nodded. "I suppose we'll take it."

"You want to go over and take a look at it first?"

"That won't be necessary." Landrum put a smile on his lean face. "We trust you, Mr. Watts. If you can't trust the town banker, who can you trust?"

Watts grinned and picked up a fat cigar which had gone out in the ashtray on his desk. He stuck the stogie in his mouth and said around it, "I wish everybody felt that way, Mr. Davis. Some folks seem to think that all bankers are dishonest, just because a few of them have been known to abscond with their depositers' savings." He leaned forward and clasped his meaty hands together. "By the way, how'd you like to open an account with us while you're here today?"

Landrum suppressed the chuckle he felt coming in.

He had never met Watts until today, but he had run into plenty of old reprobates just like him in the past. Watts was probably honest enough — as long as it suited him.

"I think we'll have to wait on that matter," Landrum said. "Maybe later, if things go well for us."

"All right. I'll have my clerk draw up the papers on the rental of that house."

Ten minutes later, several bills had changed hands and Landrum and Celia had a place to stay. They said their good-byes to Watts and started out of the office, but then Landrum paused in the doorway. Looking back at the banker, he asked, "What's the best place in town to get a drink these days?"

"Only one place," Watts replied. "O'Leary's, just down the street."

"Thanks," Landrum nodded. The thirsty look on his face as he and Celia left the bank was not there for show, or as part of their cover. The trip had been a long and dusty one, and there was nothing he wanted more right now than a cold beer and a shot of smooth whiskey.

He looked along the street when they emerged from the bank and spotted O'Leary's Shamrock Saloon on the opposite side, several doors down. It was a one-story frame building with the name of the establishment emblazoned on its false front with bright green paint. Landrum remembered it from his prior visit to Truscott. At that time, there had been another saloon in town, a little hole-in-the-wall place called Ike's. He had spent most of his drinking time there, preferring a smaller place where he could concentrate on his liquor and not be bothered.

Ike's was closed now, he saw as he and Celia started toward O'Leary's. Celia asked, "Have you been in this saloon before?"

"A couple of times," Landrum replied. "The old man who owns it has visions of grandeur that are sort of out of place around here. He had a crystal chandelier brought all the way up here from Dallas, and the bar itself came from Denver, if I remember his bragging right."

"All that for a wide place in the road like Truscott?"

Landrum shrugged. "I told you he was strange."

The Shamrock Saloon seemed to be doing a steady business, Landrum saw as he paused in the batwinged entrance. There were several cowboys standing at the bar, and a poker game was going on at one of the tables. Aloysious O'Leary himself was tending bar, a tall, spare man with thick white hair and sweeping white mustaches.

Celia drew some interested looks as she accompanied Landrum up to the bar. As he had suspected, a young woman so lovely was a rarity here on the High Plains. This was a desolate land; beauty didn't last long in these parts.

Landrum rested a palm on the smooth mahogany surface of the bar and said, "I'd like a cold beer first, then a shot of your best whiskey, Mr. O'Leary."

The Irishman started to nod, then abruptly squinted at Landrum. "Do I know ye, lad?"

"Landrum Davis. I was here in Truscott a while back, came in here a few times for a drink."

"I'm afraid I don't recall the occasions, Mr. Davis. However, I'm glad ye came back. Welcome to the Shamrock Saloon." The old men drew the beer and placed the mug on the bar in front of Landrum, then raised his bushy white brows as he glanced at Celia. "And what can I be gettin' for the young lady now?"

"Whiskey," Celia said bluntly without waiting for Landrum to answer for her. "I'll skip the beer."

O'Leary bent and took a bottle from underneath the bar. "Very well." He splashed liquor in glasses for Landrum and Celia. There was a faintly disapproving look on his lined face.

Celia picked up her glass, took a sip, then closed her eyes in satisfaction for a moment. Then she swallowed the rest of the fiery stuff. If this was an example of O'Leary's finest, she would have hated to taste the rotgut. This whiskey was raw and harsh, but the glow it started in her belly was pleasant enough.

Landrum drank half of his beer first, then downed the whiskey. He shared Celia's assessment of its quality. And chances were, the booze they were trying to track down was even worse. There wasn't a less discriminating drinker in the world than an Indian.

"I see Ike's place is closed up," Landrum said as he sipped what was left of his beer. "He decide to retire?"

"Retired six feet under, he did," O'Leary replied, leaning on the mahogany and wiping it with the ever-present bar rag. "Dropped dead one night. Heart gave out, I hear tell. Some cowhands from down 'round Munday were the only ones in there at the time. They propped 'im up behind the bar with a bottle in his hand and left him there. Gave the next customers quite a start, don't ye know?"

Landrum laughed appreciatively at the story. "So you're the only source of good drinking liquor around here now, is that it? You must be doing good business

41

these days."

"Fair," O'Leary shrugged. "The Shamrock may be the only saloon, but 'tis always a way for a man to find a drink, happen he wants one bad enough."

Landrum nodded sagely and lowered his voice. "Somebody around here running a still, is there?" he asked in conspiratorial tones.

"I wouldn't know, laddybuck. And I don't want to." The saloonkeeper cut his eyes from side to side, as if worried that someone might be listening.

Landrum pushed on rapidly, not wanting to attract too much attention with his questioning. "Well, as long as we've got you around, Mr. O'Leary, I won't worry about being able to get some good whiskey when I want it."

"You and the missus'll be staying awhile, Mr. Davis?"

Landrum glanced at Celia and grinned broadly. "Yes. Miss Burnett and I have rented the Stanley house."

O'Leary blinked. It was unusual for a man to admit so brazenly that he was living in sin with a woman. And from the looks of the lush young redhead, the living might well be sinful indeed.

Landrum drained the last of his beer and placed the empty mug on the bar. He said, "In fact, we'd better go collect our baggage and be getting home. We just came in on the stage, you know."

"Aye," O'Leary nodded. "I saw the two of ye getting off."

Landrum spun a coin onto the bar to pay for the drinks, then took Celia's arm and turned toward the door. As they walked toward the batwings, they had to pass the table where the poker game was in progress. A slick-haired man in a frock coat — obviously a professional gambler — looked up from the cards he was dealing and said to Landrum, "Care to join us for a hand or two, my friend?"

Landrum shook his head. "I don't think so."

"With so lovely a lady at your side, your luck would probably be running high."

Celia smiled at him. "Thank you, sir. I'm glad someone appreciates the way I look." She shot a venomous glance at Landrum.

One of the other players, a large, rumpled young man, grinned and said, "Shoot, lady, I appreciate the hell outta the way you look. You can come over here and sit with me if you want. I'll take all the luck I can get."

It was plain from the way his gaze roved over Celia's body that he would take anything else he could get, too. His voice cold, Landrum said, "The lady and I are leaving. Sorry."

"Wait a minute, mister." The big youngster had laid down his cards and started to get to his feet. "I asked her to sit with me. Hadn't you ought to let her answer for herself?"

Another man, who was sitting beside the one who was now facing Landrum across the table, caught at his companion's arm and said in a low voice, "Better let it go, Claude. Arlie ain't gonna like it if'n we get in a shootin' scrape."

"I won't like it either, Moody," the gambler said sharply. "Now sit back down, and let's play some cards."

Reluctantly, the big man called Claude Moody sat

43

down again. He glared after Landrum and Celia as they left the saloon.

"Well, did we plant enough seeds back there?" Celia asked as they crossed the street again, this time heading toward the stage station.

"We'll find out," Landrum said. "You can count on that."

Their bags had been unloaded from the now-departed stage, as Landrum had instructed the driver. They were waiting to be picked up on the porch of the way station. Landrum hefted the two larger bags, while Celia carried the smaller one that contained her cosmetics, a small flask of liquor, and a .38 Colt.

Landrum led her down the street and around a block to the small whitewashed frame house they had rented. It had a run-down fence around a yard full of dead grass. Landrum swung open the gate and stepped back to let Celia precede him.

"Welcome home, my dear," he said.

CHAPTER FIVE

Ration day at the fort was every Thursday. All the Indians who lived in the area would show up early, gathering in front of the Indian agent's office to wait for the week's worth of supplies they would be given. The provisions were usually barely enough to last a week, but the Indians took them anyway, accepting the meat, flour, beans, and sugar with little grace and no gratitude.

It was hard to be thankful for something that had sapped the fighting spirits of once-mighty tribes.

Like the other Indians, Gerald Glidinghawk arrived at the agent's office when the sun was just peeking over the horizon. The early morning mist had not burned away yet, and it gave the fort an eerie aspect as the wet tendrils floated over the parade ground.

He might arouse suspicion if he wasn't present for ration day, Glidinghawk had decided. Although it was certainly a degrading spectacle, he thought as he looked over the crowd of Indians waiting in front of the small frame building that housed Fox's office.

Follett's office, Glidinghawk corrected himself. All four members of Powell's Army had cover identities on this mission, but Fox was the only one with a phony name. Landrum had already been known in Truscott by his true name, so it had made no sense to come up with a false one for Celia.

And Glidinghawk's actual background fit right in with what they were hoping to accomplish—up to a point—so there had been no point in deceiving anyone about him either.

So far he hadn't run into anyone who would remember him from his days with the Omahas—the time of his abortive attempt to return to the red man's world after having been raised and educated a white. He had gone so far as to marry a half-breed squaw and father a child . . . but those had been futile gestures. He would never fit in there, and he should have seen that immediately, he had thought bitterly later. He had pulled up stakes, as Landrum would have put it—lit a shuck out of there.

But if he did encounter anyone who knew that part of his history, it would help emphasize the character he was trying to establish—a bitter, angry outcast with no morals. The type of man who would do almost anything if the price was right . . .

Glidinghawk sat on the hard ground next to the porch of the office, his back against the foundation of the building. His knees were drawn up, his arms resting loosely on them. He stared straight ahead, his face impassive, as he listened to the chatter of the women and the playful screams of the children. Some of the braves were there, but not all. Those who had squaws sent them to get the rations.

The scuff of feet made Glidinghawk glance up. Standing by the steps leading up to the office's porch were several warriors. One of them was the Kiowa with whom he had fought a few days earlier. The others were probably friends of his, judging from the way they were glaring at Glidinghawk.

A thin smile curved Glidinghawk's lips. "Come back for more, have you?" he asked.

The Kiowa's fingers trembled with anger as he said, "This time it will be to the death, dog."

"I see you brought help with you this time, too."

The Kiowa shook his head. "I need no help to deal with you. These warriors have to witness your humiliation and death."

Glidinghawk shrugged and put a hand on the ground as he started to get up. He hadn't wanted things to get this out of hand.

The Kiowa's hand flashed to his waist and came out with a knife. For an instant, Glidinghawk thought the man was going to slash at him with it, and he steeled himself for the bite of the blade. But instead, the Kiowa flung it down in front of Glidinghawk. The point stuck in the ground, and the hilt quivered from the impact.

His face grim, the Kiowa took another knife from the buckskin pants. He used it to gesture at the first weapon and said, "There. This will be a fair fight."

Glidinghawk looked down at the knife for a moment, aware that silence had fallen over the group of Indians. The women and the children stared, unsure what would happen next. The men watched with great interest. Glidinghawk had no friends here; he was sure of that.

If he was killed, no one would mourn him. No one would sing the death chants for him.

The mission would be over before it hardly began.

But he could not let this challenge go unanswered. He had too much pride for that.

Slowly, he bent over and plucked the knife from the ground.

The Kiowa grinned suddenly, anticipating his victory and Glidinghawk's death. As soon as Glidinghawk had straightened, knife in hand, the Kiowa lunged forward with a harsh cry.

Glidinghawk dodged to the side as the Kiowa cut at him. He threw his knife hand up, and the blades rang together with a clang of steel. Glidinghawk shoved hard, driving the Kiowa's weapon aside for a split second.

He could have used the opportunity to thrust his blade at his opponent's unprotected belly. Instead, Glidinghawk threw a punch with his free hand, driving his fist into the Kiowa's stomach with stunning force. The brave staggered backward from the blow, but as he did so, he chopped down at Glidinghawk's left arm with the knife.

Glidinghawk felt the line of heat and pain that the blade drew down his arm. For a few seconds, it didn't hurt too badly, but then waves of agony rippled through him. Red flames seemed to dance in front of his eyes.

He dove forward, once more knocking the Kiowa's knife to one side. His head slammed into the man's chest. Glidinghawk brought the knife up from down low, slicing at the Kiowa's body. Only a desperate twist by the man enabled him to avoid the full danger of the move. Instead of piercing his chest, the point of the blade merely ripped along the side of his body above the ribs. He yelped in pain, got his hand on Glidinghawk's chest, and shoved hard.

Glidinghawk didn't have his weight balanced, owing to the effort he had put into the thrust at the Kiowa's chest. He took a couple of unsteady steps to the side, managing to catch himself before he fell. There were several feet between the two men now, though. Both men tried to catch their breath.

His gaze flickering past the Kiowa, he saw the circle of Indians watching the fight, saw the keen interest on their faces. They would like to see him defeated, he realized, even gutted on the Kiowa's knife.

That wasn't going to happen. The man simply wasn't as good as he thought he was.

But Glidinghawk suddenly knew how close he had come to letting his rage carry him away. He had almost killed the Kiowa. Only the man's frantic speed in avoiding Glidinghawk's knife had saved his life.

Glidinghawk had killed before, and knew he probably would have to again in the future. That wasn't what gave him pause.

There was no reason to kill the Kiowa. The man was a proud, blind fool, and that was not worth dying—or killing—over.

His lips pulling back from his teeth in a grimace, Glidinghawk suddenly drew back his hand and threw the knife. The Kiowa watched impassive as the blade skewered into the ground between his feet. He knew quite well that it could have landed in his heart just as easily.

"No more," Glidinghawk said hoarsely. "I have no quarrel with you. I will not continue this foolish battle."

The Kiowa's pride would not let him back down.

49

"Pick up the knife again," he grated.

Glidinghawk shook his head and said, "No." He started to turn away.

The Kiowa watched him for a second, then his face contorting in rage at the prospect of being cheated of his revenge, he threw himself forward, knife upraised to drive into the back of the enemy.

Glidinghawk heard him coming. It was no surprise. The Omaha started to whirl around, to try to catch the man's wrist and prevent a killing.

The sudden blast of black powder made women and children scream. The Kiowa's lunge was stopped short. In fact, he bounced back slightly as if he had just run into some sort of invisible wall. The knife slipped from his fingers, and he used his hand instead to touch the hole in his chest. Blood welled out over his fingers.

He pitched forward on his face, dead, all need for vengeance gone.

Glidinghawk jerked around toward the source of the shot. Sergeant Bradley Foster angrily pushed past several jabbering squaws, the pistol in his hand still trailing wispy strands of powdersmoke from its barrel. "Out of the way, goddammit!" he snapped.

Glidinghawk drew a deep breath and faced Foster. The Omaha's face was bleak as he said. "I could have stopped him without killing him."

Foster snorted. "Looked to me like he was about carve you up good. Reckon I'm sorry I tried to save your life." The noncom's face was brick-red with anger.

Glidinghawk made a conscious effort to relax. He said, "I appreciate what you did, Sergeant." He lifted his left arm, the sleeve of his buckskins soaked with blood from the gash. "I might not have been able to

50

handle him after all."

From the porch of the Indian agent's office, Preston Fox shouted, "My God! What's happened here?" Obviously, his attention had been drawn by the shot just outside the building.

Foster jammed his pistol back in its holster. "Had to shoot one of the Indians," he told Fox. "There was a fight, and that brave on the ground was about to stab this one in the back." The sergeant nodded to Glidinghawk to indicate who he was talking about.

Fox's eyes met Glidinghawk's for an instant, and the Omaha gave a minuscule nod to confirm Foster's statement. Fox's face was pale as he looked at the motionless form of the dead Kiowa. "I . . . I suppose you did what you had to do, Sergeant," he said. "Fill out a report for your commanding officer, and he can pass it on to me."

"Yes, sir," Foster replied, his tone barely civil. He didn't like being talked to that way by a civilian, Glidinghawk could tell.

"And you," Fox's sharp words lashed at Glidinghawk, "you come into my office. I want to have a word with you."

Foster quickly stepped up onto the porch. He lowered his voice, but Glidinghawk could still hear him as he said, "I don't know if that's a good idea, sir. That one seems to be a troublemaker, he does."

Fox gave the sergeant a cold stare. "I thought you were going to give him a lesson in manners."

"Maybe it didn't take," Foster replied between gritted teeth. "Maybe I should try again."

Fox shook his head. "Not this time. I want to talk to him. I'm certain I'll be all right, Sergeant. A fight between savages is one thing. No Indian is going to attempt to attack me with the fort and the troops right here."

Foster looked dubious, but he stepped back and gestured for Glidinghawk to come up onto the porch. Glidinghawk went up the steps with his face emotionless.

The burly supply sergeant prodded a blunt finger into Glidinghawk's chest. "You behave yourself," he said. "If you don't, you'll wind up like your friend there."

Glidinghawk glanced at the dead Kiowa. There were no women hovering over him, so evidently he had no wife, at least not here. Glidinghawk had suspected as much. The man's companions were gathered around his body, all of them sending hate-filled glances Glidinghawk's way.

"He wasn't my friend," Glidinghawk said bluntly. "But I understand what you mean, Sergeant."

"See that you do." Foster barked orders at the Kiowa's friends to get the body out of there, then he turned back to Fox and said, "We can start giving out the rations as soon as you're ready, Mr. Follett."

"Very well. It shouldn't take long to deal with this fellow, and then we'll get on with it."

Fox motioned curtly for Glidinghawk to follow him, then went into the anteroom and on through into the office beyond. He sank wearily into the chair behind his desk as Glidinghawk stood stiffly in front of him.

"Oh, relax, dammit," Fox said as he glanced up at Glidinghawk. "Sit down." His voice was pitched too low to be heard outside the office, and the window behind him was closed.

Glidinghawk pulled a ladder-backed chair up and sat down. He said, "I thought you brought me in here to lay down the law to me."

Fox leaned forward and clasped his hands together. Now that they were alone, his air of self-confidence had faded somewhat. "What happened out there?" he asked.

"What Foster said. The Kiowa picked a fight. I lost my head for a minute and almost killed him myself. But it was over as far as I was concerned. The Kiowa thought differently."

"And Foster had to shoot him?"

Glidinghawk shrugged. "Had to? Maybe not. But there's no doubt the brave was really trying to kill me."

"All right," Fox said with a nod. "Have you come any closer to finding out who the whiskey smugglers are working with here?"

The Omaha shook his head. "We've made it plain that I'm a loner, and a violent one at that. But no one has approached me yet."

"What now?"

Glidinghawk didn't reply for a moment while he thought over Fox's question. They couldn't do anything too blatant, or that would tip their hand.

Finally, he said, "All we can do is continue on the way we're going. But there may be a way to place me even more firmly on the other side."

"How's that?"

"Everyone thinks that I'm in trouble with the Indian agent since you made me come in here. Let's give them even more cause to think so."

"How are we going to do that?"

Glidinghawk suppressed a smile and began to explain. As he did so, Fox's face became more and more disapproving. By the time Glidinghawk was through sketching out the plan, Fox looked downright distressed.

"You're sure about this?" the young man asked.

"I'm sure," Glidinghawk nodded.

"Well . . . all right."

Glidinghawk stood up and went to the door. Fox followed him, raising his voice in an angry warning for Glidinghawk to stay out of trouble. As Fox yanked the door of the building open, he said, "And the next time, you'll wind up in the stockade! I can promise you that, you filthy redskin!"

Sullenly, Glidinghawk pushed past Fox and walked away from the agent's office with a stiff back, anger radiating from him. He could feel eyes watching him, but he didn't look around to see who they belonged to.

Perhaps this next step would bear fruit, Glidinghawk thought. He hoped so.

CHAPTER SIX

Glidinghawk kept to himself the rest of the day. He drew his rations with the other Indians, then found a place behind a storage shed to brood.

Some of the attitude was a pose—but not all of it. This assignment was getting to him. Being around the reservation Indians all the time was too painful a reminder of his own past.

But his job was to find out who was smuggling whiskey into the Territory, and no matter how long it took to accomplish that end, he would continue with the ruse.

The next morning dawned gray and gloomy, with spring thunderstorms rumbling in the west. Appropriate weather considering his mood, Glidinghawk thought as he tried to stretch some of the stiffness out of his muscles and bones. It wasn't raining yet, but it probably would be before the day was over.

At midmorning, he was slouching past the Indian agent's office, his head down, his eyes on the ground. He heard the door of the office bang open, and out of the corner of his eye, he saw Preston Fox hurry across the porch and come down the steps. Fox seemed to be intent on whatever errand he was on. The young man paid no attention as he started across the parade ground toward the headquarters building.

Glidinghawk ran right into him.

The two men bumped hard. Glidinghawk was larger, but Fox was going faster. Both of them were staggered by the collision. Fox lost his balance and went to one knee.

"Damn you, Indian!" he yelped as he leaped back to his feet and started brushing his pants off. "Can't you watch where you're going, you stupid heathen?"

Glidinghawk glanced across the parade ground. There were plenty of Indians around this morning, but more importantly, there were dozens of soldiers to witness the confrontation.

With a surly sneer on his face, Glidinghawk faced Fox and said, "You ran into me, Mr. Indian Agent. It was your fault."

"My fault!" Fox exclaimed. "Why, that's preposterous! You're to blame, redskin, and I demand an apology forthwith."

Careful, Preston, Glidinghawk thought. Don't make it so ridiculous that no one will believe it.

"I will not apologize," the Omaha declared, letting his voice raise slightly. "Another fool made the mistake of thinking me a white man's dog."

Fox grimaced. "I haven't forgotten about that fight mister, or the fact that one of your fellow savages wound up dead. That was your fault, too."

Glidinghawk waved an arm at Fox. "Just leave me alone."

"I will not!" Fox's voice was shrill and carrying. "I warned you just yesterday to stay out of trouble." He reached to grab Glidinghawk's arm. "Come along with

56

me! We'll see the commanding officer and have you tossed in the stockade! Maybe that will teach you a lesson."

Glidinghawk stiffened as Fox grasped his arm. "Let me go," he warned in a dangerous voice. "I will not be caged like an animal."

"That's what you are!" Fox tugged on him. "Come along!"

With a guttural, wordless shout, Glidinghawk tore his arm out of Fox's fingers. Before Fox could stop him, Glidinghawk pivoted and brought his fist around in a short, powerful blow. The Omaha's knuckles smacked into Fox's jaw, driving him backward.

Fox lost his balance and sat down hard in the dirt.

One of the nearby soldiers, who had been watching during the exchange of angry words, now yelled "Hey!" and started forward to help Fox.

Fox threw his hand out to stop the man. "No!" he called. "I'll handle this!"

The young man came to his feet, his eyes slightly glassy. He faced Glidinghawk with a furious look on his face. "You've made a big mistake, redskin," he grated. "I'm going to give you the thrashing of your life!"

Another trooper, gauging the relative sizes of Fox and Glidinghawk, started to say, "Sir, wait—" but it was too late. Fox lunged at the Omaha, throwing a wild, looping punch.

Glidinghawk could have avoided the blow completely, but as he dodged aside he moved slowly enough to let Fox's fist clip him on the side of the head. They had to make this look real—otherwise it would do no good.

Fox hadn't liked the idea very much, but Gliding-hawk had to give him credit—at least he was trying to go through with it.

Glidinghawk slammed a hard, knobby fist into his belly.

Air gusted out of Fox. His face turned pale, but he had the presence of mind to keep up the act. He drove another punch at Glidinghawk's face. Glidinghawk took this one full on the cheek, knowing it didn't have enough power behind it to seriously damage him.

He blocked Fox's next punch, grabbed his arm, and pulled him close to grapple with him. Locked together, the two men swayed in the effort to topple each other.

His mouth close to Fox's ear, Glidinghawk hissed, "You're doing fine, Preston!"

Fox just grunted in pain and genuine anger. Glid-inghawk ducked his head and butted it against Fox so that no one would see the grin that flickered across his features.

They fell heavily, Glidinghawk landing on top. He brought his knee up, being careful to hit Fox on the thigh rather than in the groin. To the crowd of shout-ing men who were watching the fight, though, it would look like an honest miss.

Glidinghawk was aware of the soldiers. They had formed a tight circle around him and Fox. The Indians were watching, too, but they were staying farther back. Glidinghawk wasn't sure who the soldiers were rooting for. Fox was an arrogant prig in real life—at least some of the time—and he had adopted that same personality in his cover identity.

Although they would deny it, some of the troopers were probably hoping that Glidinghawk would beat the hell out of the new Indian agent.

Fox summoned his strength and heaved his body up, throwing Glidinghawk off him. He tried to make use of the momentary advantage as Glidinghawk rolled to one side in the dirt, but the Omaha recovered too quickly. As Fox leaped at him, Glidinghawk managed to lift his moccasined feet.

Fox's stomach hit Glidinghawk's feet, and he suddenly found himself cartwheeling and flying through the air over the Omaha. He yelled in fear, a shrieking sound abruptly cut off as he crashed to the ground on his back.

Glidinghawk rolled over and sprang to his feet, ready to continue the fight if need be. He saw immediately that it wouldn't be necessary. Fox was sprawled in the dirt, gasping for air and moaning.

Shocked silence fell over the crowd. Then, cutting through the quiet, came the sound of a pistol being cocked.

The noncoms and enlisted men suddenly snapped to attention as Colonel Lawrence Selmon came striding through the crowd. The colonel had his pistol out and leveled at Glidinghawk.

"Take that Indian into custody!" Selmon snapped.

A couple of sergeants sprang forward to follow the order. They grasped Glidinghawk's arms tightly and held him motionless. Selmon stalked up to him with a fierce glare.

"You'll regret this incident, Indian," the colonel said. "Some time in the stockade will teach you a little humility."

A sergeant spoke up, and Glidinghawk saw that it was Bradley Foster. "Beggin' the colonel's pardon, sir, but it looked to me like Mr. Follet started this little ruckus himself."

Selmon shook his head. "That doesn't matter, Sergeant. We will not have savages assaulting white men, regardless of the cause. Take him away," he added to the men holding Glidinghawk.

Glidinghawk allowed them to jerk him into motion, but before he went, he spat contemptuously in the dirt at Selmon's feet. He just had time to see the brick-red flush of anger on the commanding officer's face before he was being hustled toward the squat, rock building that served as the fort's stockade.

The plan appeared to have worked. The whole fort would know now what a renegade he was. The only question was whether or not it had worked too well.

He couldn't do Powell's Army a damned bit of good as long as he was locked up.

There wasn't a muscle in his body that didn't hurt, Preston Fox thought as he sat in Colonel Selmon's office a little later. The officer was glaring across the desk at him, and that didn't help Fox's feelings much either.

"I don't know what you were thinking about out there, Mr. Follett," Selmon snapped as he rustled some papers together. "How do you think it looks for an Indian agent — an employee of the federal government — to be brawling like a common enlisted man with one of those savages?"

Tightly, Fox answered, "The buck was impertinent to me, sir, not to mention threatening. I didn't feel that it would be wise to back down. That might have established a bad precedent and led to more trouble in the future."

"Well," Selmon grunted, "you sure didn't put the fear of God into anybody by getting the stuffing beaten out of you." The colonel shook his head. "I know how frustrating it can be trying to deal with these people, Follett. It's hard enough just getting along with Washington. But you've got to learn how to handle yourself better."

"Yes, sir," Fox said, nodding his head and keeping his features carefully expressionless.

Inside, he was seething.

It was bad enough that Glidinghawk had been so rough with him, but now he was having to endure this dressing-down by Colonel Selmon as well. When the Omaha had first outlined his plan, Fox had thought they would each throw a few punches and miss most of the time. He hadn't realized what a brutal charade it would be.

Why, he could have actually been hurt!

Taking chances was just part of being an undercover agent, he supposed. It did seem like the danger should have come from the enemy, however, not one's partner.

Selmon took out a cigar and lit it. Fox noticed that the colonel didn't offer him one of the stogies. Blowing smoke toward the ceiling, Selmon said, "You're not under my direct command, Follett, but I strongly suggest that you pay more attention in the future to doing your job. You're not going to change these Indians overnight, and you're sure as hell not going to make them respect you by wrestling around in the dirt with them. Do I make myself clear?"

Fox swallowed the bitter taste in his mouth. "Yes,

sir. Perfectly clear."

"Good. Now, we'll keep this Glidinghawk fellow in the stockade for a few days. By the time he comes out, he won't be interested in causing any more trouble for you. There's nothing an Indian hates worse than being cooped up."

Fox nodded. "Very good, sir."

"All right, you can go. But remember what I told you."

Fox stood up, his cheeks burning with resentment at the tone in the colonel's voice. Glidinghawk had really placed him in a bad position, but there was nothing he could do about it now.

There was a fresh rumble of thunder as Fox left the headquarters building. He glanced at the western sky and saw the black clouds scudding through it. Lightning flickered here and there in the thick dark mass. Although the storm was moving quickly, the winds that gave it its impetus had not yet reached the fort.

Here where Fox stood, there was only the faintest of breezes, barely strong enough to sway the flag that hung limply from the pole on the parade ground. The air was heavy, somehow electric.

Something was going to happen.

Fox gave a slight shudder, placed his hat on his head, and started back to his office.

The rain started about the middle of the afternoon. Glidinghawk heard it pounding on the roof of the stockade and wished he was outside so that he could let the torrent wash down over him.

Maybe it would remove some of the stink that

seemed to have permeated his entire being.

He sat on the packed earth of the floor with his back against the hard rock wall. The cell he was in had one small, high window, barred of course, and there was another tiny window in the heavy wooden door that led out. The cell was six feet by eight feet — not very big to start with, and it seemed to grow smaller as the day went on.

The light coming through the window diminished as the storm moved in with its thick gray clouds. Glidinghawk heard the far-off rumble of thunder, and then the rain began a few minutes later. The thunder became louder, some of the booming claps shaking the ground underneath him.

He breathed shallowly, quickly. God, he hated being locked up!

No one had come to see him since he had been thrown in here. He had no idea how long he would be left here. They would have to feed him sometime, but they would probably wait until evening mess.

No one had been seriously hurt in the scuffle with Fox. Glidinghawk couldn't believe that the colonel would order him locked up for more than a day or two. Just long enough to teach the heathen a lesson. That was the way Selmon would think.

On the other hand, the colonel might have decided to make an example of him, a warning to the other Indians to stay in line. He might be left in here for weeks, perhaps as long as a month.

And where would that leave the assignment? In that case, Fox would be left hanging, free to operate as he saw fit.

That was a frightening possibility.

The cell became almost completely dark as the hours wore on toward evening. Night fell early, and still Glidinghawk was left sitting there alone, unfed. He dozed. There was nothing else to do.

A footstep outside the cell made his head jerk up. He blinked rapidly, trying to force himself back to alertness. A key scraped in the lock of the door, and Glidinghawk winced as it swung open and the light from a lantern spilled into the room.

A dark, bulky figure loomed behind the lantern. Over the sound of the rain, Glidinghawk heard a familiar voice say, "Well, redskin, you about ready to get out of here?"

CHAPTER SEVEN

Glidinghawk tensed as he squinted past the light at Sergeant Bradley Foster. The burly noncom seemed to be alone, and he had no weapon in his other hand. The lantern was all he was carrying.

When the Omaha made no reply, Foster said impatiently, "I asked you a question, Glidinghawk. You may not know it, but I'm here to help you."

Slowly, Glidinghawk said, "I have seen how the white man helps the Indians."

"Dammit, I ain't here to argue with you. Now, the guards are taking a break out of the rain for a smoke and a drink, courtesy of yours truly, but they ain't going to take forever to do it. If you want out, you come with me now."

Glidinghawk came to his feet, moving somewhat stiffly from sitting motionless for so long. He stepped closer to Foster and peered into the man's face.

"Why are you doing this for me?" he asked.

"Because I figure you and me can help each other out. If you ain't interested, you can sit here in this hole and rot for all I care."

Glidinghawk shook his head. If this was what he suspected it was, he didn't want to appear too eager. "I

65

will be out soon. They wouldn't lock me up for long just because I got into a fight."

"A fight with an Indian agent," Foster reminded him. "And the way I hear it, Selmon intends to keep you in here for at least a month. That what you want, dammit?" The sergeant's tone was becoming more impatient by the second.

Glidinghawk took a deep breath. "All right," he said. "I couldn't stand that."

"Didn't figure you could. Come on."

Following closely behind Foster, Glidinghawk went down the narrow corridor leading past the several cells in the stockade building. Another heavy door with iron straps barred the far end of the corridor. Beyond it was freedom.

Foster pushed it open and paused long enough to peer out into the rainy night. He had already extinguished the lantern. Glidinghawk could barely see him as he jerked his head and hissed, "Come on!"

Quickly, the two men emerged from the building. Instantly, Glidinghawk's buckskins were soaked. Rainwater streamed through his hair and dripped into his eyes. He stayed close behind Foster, not wanting to get separated from the sergeant who had freed him.

The thunder and lightning had moved on for the most part, although there was an occasional flicker and rumble from far away. The storm had left behind plenty of rain, however. It was a downpour, a physical obstacle through which Foster and Glidinghawk had to push their way.

More shapes loomed up out of the darkness. Glidinghawk heard the nervous whickers and recognized them as horses. They were tired to one of the hitch racks in front of the now-closed sutler's store. Foster yanked the reins loose and put his mouth close to Glidinghawk's ear. "I'll lead them out of the fort," he said. "We'll mount up then."

Glidinghawk nodded. He put a hand on the flank of one of the animals and let it remain there to keep himself oriented. Within moments, he and Foster had slipped through one of the gates and were outside the fort.

They had not been challenged by sentries, and Glidinghawk wondered if Foster had paid these guards off, too. That was possible, but it was also possible that the sentries had simply missed them in this rain. Foster could have been counting on that.

When they were several yards away from the fort, Foster called softly, "All right. Mount up."

Glidinghawk reached up, found the pommel of the military saddle, and hauled himself aboard the horse. It danced skittishly to the side, but Glidinghawk kept a firm hand on the reins and calmed it.

"Stay close," Foster advised him. Glidinghawk had been doing just that. He urged the horse into motion alongside Foster's mount.

As they rode through the night, Glidinghawk considered the events that had occurred. He felt certain that Foster had something to do with the whiskey smuggling. He couldn't think of any other reason for the sergeant to help him escape from the stockade. Foster wasn't doing it out of any love for Indians, Glidinghawk thought. He had never demonstrated any great affection for the inhabitants of the reservations.

Likewise, Foster didn't seem to have much respect for the army in general. He was just the type of man who would be involved in a scheme to smuggle liquor into a prohibited territory.

From the beginning, Glidinghawk's troublesome behavior had been calculated to attract the attention of just such a man. If the ruse had been successful, the whiskey runners might think he was a man who would come in handy for their plans.

He and Foster rode for what seemed hours through the rain. The downpour slacked off after a while, dwindling to a steady drizzle rather than a torrent. Glidinghawk could see a little better now, and he realized that Foster wore an oilskin slicker.

The sergeant had not seen fit to provide him with one, Glidinghawk mused. He was as wet and miserable as a soaked rat. Grimly, he wondered if Colonel Amos Powell and his missions were worth all this trouble.

He knew the answer to that, though. Glidinghawk was no judge of how important it was to keep whiskey out of the Indian Nations. Such considerations were not really his business.

Doing a job — and doing it well — that was what mattered to him. He had drifted aimlessly for years. Now Powell — and Landrum and Celia and, yes, even Fox — they were his anchors.

Which was a damned appropriate thought, he realized with a bleak smile, considering the fact that the storm had turned every low place in the ground into a lake.

The rain softened to a mist and finally stopped altogether. Glidinghawk estimated that at least an hour had passed since they had slipped away from the fort. He had no idea where they were or even what direction they had been riding. But as the clouds began to shred and blow away overhead, Glidinghawk caught a glimpse of the stars. Judging from the pinpoints of light, he thought that they had probably been heading southwest, deeper into the Nations.

A quarter-moon appeared, casting a silver glow over the puddles. Glidinghawk saw Foster hold up a hand in a signal to stop. The noncom said, "Hold it. We'd best be careful now."

They went forward at a slow walk on the horses. Glidinghawk thought he spotted something up ahead, and as they approached, the dim shape turned into something recognizable — a wagon pulled by a team of mules. One man was waiting on the seat, and two more sat close by on horseback.

All of them had rifles in their hands. Glidinghawk saw moonlight glinting off the barrels.

"It's me, Arlie," Foster called softly.

One of the men on horseback lifted his rifle and replied, "Who's that with you?"

"The fella I told you about. Glidinghawk."

"Come ahead," the stranger grunted.

Foster's horse stepped closer to the wagon. Glidinghawk rode closely behind him. Peering through the shadows, he could see the barrels in the back of the wagon.

Whiskey barrels, Glidinghawk thought.

The first objective of the mission had been accomplished.

Now came the hard part.

Glidinghawk could see how the man called Arlie kept his rifle barrel angled toward him. Evidently the man was plenty suspicious. Not surprising, considering his line of work.

"That's far enough," Arlie said as Glidinghawk and Foster rode closer. The man was a large, bulky shape in the darkness owing to the buffalo coat he wore. The rain-soaked garment gave off a pungent odor that drifted to Glidinghawk's nose.

The man on the wagon seat said, "I ain't sure 'bout this, Arlie. Don't much like workin' with a redskin."

"Shut up, Benton," Arlie snapped. "I been makin' the decisions for the family for a long time, and I ain't about to turn the job over to you now."

Benton snorted. "You make the decisions, huh? I'll be sure an' tell Ma about that."

Arlie twisted in the saddle. "I told you to shut up! Who you think Ma's goin' to believe, you or me?"

The wagon driver, probably Arlie's brother from the sound of it, subsided, contenting himself with muttering a few surly comments. Arlie turned his attention back to Glidinghawk and Foster.

"Ain't happy about this weather," Arlie growled to Foster. "It sure come a frog-strangler. Damn near washed us away."

"Well, you're here, and that's what matters," Foster replied. "Did you manage to make all the deliveries so far?"

"Sure. Got just a few more stops to make north of here." Arlie reached inside his heavy coat and pulled out a small leather pouch. He tossed it to Foster, who caught it deftly. "There's your cut. Reckon you did your part again. We ain't seen no patrols."

Foster nodded. He didn't open the pouch, but he weighed it for a moment in his hand, then grunted in satisfaction. Inclining his head toward the Omaha, he asked, "You goin' to take Glidinghawk along with you?"

Arlie prodded his horse forward, drawing up close beside Glidinghawk. The Indian kept his face impassive and showed no reaction as the unkempt whiskey runner stared intently at him. Arlie hissed, "Reckon I can trust you, boy?"

Glidinghawk didn't answer for a long moment. Then he said, "I will do what you say, white man — as long as there is something in it for me."

"Glidinghawk won't give you any trouble," Foster assured Arlie. "He just broke out of the stockade at Fort Supply tonight. He's a fugitive, wanted now for escapin' custody as well as for assaultin' an Indian agent. Ain't that right, Glidinghawk?"

The Omaha gave an expressive shrug and remained silent.

Arlie poked the barrel of his rifle toward Glidinghawk for emphasis as he said, "I'll give you a chance, boy, but you cross me and you'll wish you was back in that stockade. Because I'll pure-dee skin ya alive and make sure you're a long time dyin'. Understand?"

"I understand," Glidinghawk said flatly.

"All right," Arlie nodded. "My name's Arlie Moody, and anybody in north Texas or the Nations 'll tell you I'm a ring-tailed bastard with all the bark still on. This here's my brother Benton" — he jerked a thumb at the man on the wagon seat — "and that feller over there is my brother Dirk. They're damn near as tough as me, and there's two more back home just like 'em. You get on the bad side of one Moody, you got to deal with all of us. You remember that."

Dirk Moody spoke for the first time from the back

of his horse. "And our ma's probably the roughest of all of us. Ain't that right, Arlie?"

"Could be," Arlie grunted. "Now listen close, Injun. Me and Dirk are headin' back across the river to Texas. You ride along with Benton whilst he drops off them last barrels of whiskey. He'll tell you what to do then. Reckon you can handle that?"

Glidinghawk nodded.

Arlie Moody patted the barrel of his rifle and gave Glidinghawk a long, pointed look. "Be seein' you," he said.

Then he and Dirk spurred their horses into motion, heading them south toward the Red River and Texas beyond.

Glidinghawk glanced at Foster as Benton Moody turned the wagon team and got them into motion. Glidinghawk said, "This is why you shot that Kiowa. You planned this."

"Didn't see any point in lettin' you die when you might be able to help all of us out," Foster admitted. "I was just waitin' for you to get yourself in deep enough. You're on the run now, Glidinghawk. You go along with us, everything will be fine. Cause any trouble and we can turn you back over to the army."

"I know a few things now about you that might prove embarrassing," Glidinghawk pointed out.

Foster shrugged and grinned. "Hell, you're a runaway Injun. I'll just shoot you, if need be. Nobody would ask one question about it, I can promise you that."

Glidinghawk knew the sergeant was right. He allowed a small smile to pass across his face. "I will cooperate," he said. "I'm not a stupid man, Sergeant

72

Foster."

"Never thought you was."

Benton Moody turned around on the wagon seat and yelled, "Hey, Injun! You comin' or not?"

"I'm coming," Glidinghawk called back to him.

Foster raised a hand in farewell as Glidinghawk put his horse into an easy trot. Glidinghawk didn't look back as he rode up next to the wagon with its load of whiskey. He glanced at the barrels in the moonlight, saw that there were four of them. From the looks of the wagon's bed, there was room there for at least half a dozen more. The biggest part of the night's work had already been done.

Sending him along for the remainder of the deliveries was a test for him, he realized. If he went along and helped Benton Moody, the clan of whiskey smugglers would probably add him to their group and use him as a regular guard on these runs.

The wagon wheels made sucking sounds as they rolled through the puddles of mud that dotted the flats. Benton looked up at Glidinghawk and asked, "You got a gun, Injun?"

Glidinghawk shook his head. "I had to leave Fort Supply in a bit of a hurry. There was no time to acquire a weapon."

"What the hell? You some kind of educated Injun?"

Glidinghawk smiled thinly and said, "I went to college at Dartmouth. That's a university back East."

" 'Course it is," Benton snapped. "You think I ain't heard of this here Dart-mouth?" Before Glidinghawk could answer that question, Benton twisted on the seat and reached into the back of the wagon. He came up with a coiled shell belt and a Sharps carbine. Extend-

73

ing them to Glidinghawk he said, "Reckon you could use these if you needed to?"

The Omaha took the weapons, slid the Colt from its holster, and spun the cylinder. It was unloaded. He began stuffing cartridges from the belt into it. "I can use them," he said.

"Good. I ain't expectin' any trouble, but you never know what you'll run into up here in the Nations."

That was the truth, Glidinghawk thought. He glanced back over his shoulder. Foster had disappeared in the shadows, no doubt heading back to Fort Supply.

Glidinghawk faced forward. Another step taken, he mused. He was that much closer to the final objective.

That much closer to a showdown.

CHAPTER EIGHT

Benton Moody proved not to be the most talkative companion Glidinghawk had ever had. He drove the wagon in sullen silence.

The clouds continued to break up as the storm moved farther east, until most of the sky above the two men was clear and starry. The silver glow from moon and stars gave the plains an eerie look.

Glidinghawk didn't think a few questions would be out of line. After all, he had a stake in this operation now.

"Where are we going?" he asked.

"Got to drop this whiskey off," Benton replied. "One barrel's goin' to a bunch of your red brothers that'll meet us. Them others we'll leave at a roadhouse a ways north of here. Feller who owns the place will keep some of it for his customers and pass the rest of it on to some of our other buyers. He gets a cut, too."

Glidinghawk nodded. The more he could learn about the scheme, the better. "And my job is to make sure no one tries to steal the whiskey, is that right?"

"Yep. There's plenty of folks who'd like to get their hands on this here load of corn squeezin's." Benton's voice took on a more aggrieved tone as he went on, "don't know why Arlie decided to leave it up to you to help me this time. He don't usually take any chances with this stuff."

"Like the sergeant says, I'm a fugitive. I can't afford to try a double-cross."

Benton snorted. "Hell, you could bust my skull with that carbine barrel, steal the whiskey, and sell it for enough to get you clear out of the Territory. That's why I'm keepin' my eye on you, boy."

Everything Benton was saying had already occurred to Glidinghawk. He didn't doubt the sincerity of Benton's nervousness. An edgy man could be dangerous—Benton wouldn't need much of an excuse to grab his gun and start blazing away. Glidinghawk knew he would have to be careful.

They rode on for maybe an hour. There were few landmarks here, just gently rolling plains with an occasional small tree. A chilly breeze blew against Glidinghawk's back, making him uncomfortably aware of his still-wet buckskins. He would be lucky if he didn't catch a cold, he thought.

The sudden appearance of several dark figures on horseback up ahead made him forget about such minor worries. He hauled in on the reins as Benton pulled the wagon to a stop. The riders were sitting motionless about fifty yards ahead of them. One of the men suddenly raised his arm above his head and waved it. There was something in his hand.

"That's the signal," Benton said. "Them's the redskins that are supposed to meet us."

Glidinghawk squinted through the darkness. "Is that a war lance he's holding?"

"Yeah." Benton cast a quick grin up at him. "These ain't no reservation Injuns like you, boy. These are the real things, and they like their firewater." He flapped the lines against the backs of the mules and got the wagon moving again.

As Glidinghawk and Benton approached the waiting Indians, the Omaha saw that they rode the squatty little mustangs that could seemingly run forever when they had to. There were five men, all of them carrying lances and wearing feathered headdresses. Cheyenne dog soldiers, maybe. Despite Benton's claim to the contrary, Glidinghawk had a feeling that they had lived on the reservation and might still return there from time to time, when the life of a renegade got too hard.

Benton brought the wagon to a halt again and held up one hand in the universal gesture of peace. He said, "Howdy, boys. Got your hooch for you here."

One of the Cheyenne poked his lance toward Glidinghawk. "Who this redskin, Moody?" he asked in guttural English.

"Just a new helper of ours," Benton explained. "Nobody for you to worry about."

A second Indian sneered at Glidinghawk and said, "Slave of white man."

Glidinghawk shook his head. "I am no slave," he said sharply. He rested his hand on the butt of the Colt.

"Here now!" Benton admonished him. "No fightin' amongst yourselves. We're here to do a job, Glidinghawk, not to get in a ruckus."

Glidinghawk nodded, but he kept his face hard and unfriendly as he watched the dog soldiers.

Benton rolled one of the barrels out of the back of the wagon. One of the Cheyenne was pulling a travois behind his horse, and two more braves quickly loaded the whiskey onto it. The one who had spoken first, who seemed to be their leader, pulled a pouch from the waistband of his buckskin pants. As Arlie Moody had done earlier with Sergeant Foster, the Indian tossed the payment to Benton.

Benton caught the pouch, opened it, and poured coins into his hand. A grin spread across his face. "Thanks, Chief," he said. "Now, you remember what Arlie said about next time. Two barrels for five squaws."

"We remember," the Cheyenne nodded.

A corner of Glidinghawk's mouth twitched. They were not only selling the rotgut for money, no doubt obtained by selling off goods that the Indians stole on their raids, but they were also trading the whiskey for women.

If the squaws were fairly young, there would be a market for them as slaves and prostitutes. Glidinghawk had seen situations like this before, and they had never failed to stir an icy-cold anger inside him.

For all he knew, his wife could be lying down with anybody who had the coins by now. It was not unheard of among the reservation Indians, although the women who sold themselves were always looked down on. Glidinghawk felt a sickening twist in his belly as the thought crossed his mind.

The transaction completed, the Cheyenne turned their horses and rode west, taking the whiskey with them. There was probably a camp of renegades up there in the panhandle somewhere to which they would return. Then there would be plenty of drinking and celebrating and, ultimately, more raids on the white settlements down in Texas.

Benton watched the Indians until they vanished into the shadows, then climbed back onto the wagon. "We'd best get movin'," he said. "It's gettin' late, and ol' Donaldson will be waitin' for us."

Glidinghawk did not ask who Donaldson was, figuring that was the name of the man who ran the roadhouse Benton had mentioned. He fell in beside the wagon as the vehicle angled northeast.

Glidinghawk studied the stars again and tried to figure out what time it was. It seemed like hours since he and Foster had left Fort Supply, and when he thought about it, he decided that it was still a good while until midnight.

Still, it was a long way back to the Red River. If the Moodys' headquarters was located across the border in Texas, it would be at late the next day at the earliest before they could reach it, maybe longer depending on exactly where it was.

He suddenly spotted a light twinkling far ahead of them. Leveling a finger at the pinprick of illumination, Glidinghawk asked, "Is that where we're headed?"

"That's Donaldson's, all right. He always leaves a light on for us." Benton laughed shortly. "He don't want us missin' him in the dark. 'Thout whiskey, he'd have to close up and go back to workin' for a livin'."

As they drew closer, Glidinghawk saw that the roadhouse was a low, rambling structure of adobe and rough planks. There was no sign on the building announcing what it was; the people who lived in these parts would know without one. Chances were the man operating the tavern was in the Territory illegally. Even though this was known as Indian Territory, so many whites had moved in that the army made only a token effort to keep them out.

Eventually, Glidinghawk knew, the government would have no choice but to open the entire Territory for settlement by the whites. When that day came, more of the so-called solemn treaties would be discarded, and the Indians would be forced to move on.

The door of the roadhouse opened as Benton drove up in front of it, spilling more light out into the night. A voice called from inside, "That you, Moody?"

"It's me, all right, Donaldson," Benton replied. "Put that greener up 'fore you hurt somebody."

A thick-bodied man of medium height moved into the doorway. He was holding a short-barreled shotgun, and he kept the twin muzzles of the weapon pointing in the general direction of the newcomers as he asked, "Who's that with you?"

"New man that Arlie plans on usin' to help us," Benton said. "He's an Injun name of—"

"My name is not important," Glidinghawk cut in brusquely. There was no point in taking foolish chances. He didn't want to get caught up in this mission and then suddenly have an army patrol show up looking for him. Best to keep his trail hidden as much as possible.

"Yeah," Benton put in. "His name ain't important. What matters is that he's goin' to help us unload this here load of liquor for you, Donaldson."

"Well, get at it, then," the roadhouse owner said. "You're late, and I want to get to bed."

"Come on, Injun. Let's roll them barrels out."

Glidinghawk dismounted while Benton got down from the wagon. Quickly, they wrestled a barrel of rotgut out of the wagon bed and on into the building. Donaldson stepped back out of the doorway to let them through, and Glidinghawk saw in the light from the lantern inside that he was a middle-aged man with a mostly bald pate. A fringe of graying red hair rode above his ears. His face was freckled, and there were large liver spots on the backs of his hands. He held the scattergun with a casual confidence.

Inside, the roadhouse was one big, low-ceilinged room. A blanket hung from a rope across the back of the room, closing off a small area where Donaldson probably slept. There was a rude bar made from planks laid across empty barrels, a few rough-hewn tables, a scattering of ladder-back chairs. A short, heavyset, round-faced squaw stood behind the bar, her features stolid. She paid no attention to Glidinghawk and Benton. She was the only one in the place besides Donaldson.

"Put 'er over there behind the bar," Donaldson told them. He cradled the shotgun in his arms and stood to one side of the door.

Glidinghawk and Benton moved the heavy barrel behind the bar. The squaw still didn't look at them. Benton said to Donaldson, "I reckon you got the money."

"Sure. You boys are the best source of whiskey I've ever had. I ain't goin' to try to cheat you." The man grinned, showing yellowed stumps of teeth. "I'm a mite surprised to see you workin' with an Injun, Benton. You always said you couldn't stand their stink."

"I just do what Arlie tells me to," Benton grunted. "Long as I get my share of the money, I don't give a damn who I work with."

Donaldson glanced at the impassive squaw. "Yeah, and you c'n get used to a stink, if you have to. Ain't that right, woman?"

She nodded slowly, ponderously.

Glidinghawk would be glad when they got out of here. He didn't like this place, didn't like Donaldson.

He and Benton had just started toward the door to get the second barrel when the sudden pound of hoofbeats outside made them stiffen. Donaldson turned quickly toward the door, hefting the shotgun in readiness again. Benton jerked his head at Glidinghawk, indicating that they should separate. They spread out, Glidinghawk going to the right, Benton to the left.

Glidinghawk glanced over his shoulder. The squaw was slowly sinking behind the barrels that formed the bar, in case there was any gunfire.

The hoofbeats came to a stop outside. Glidinghawk heard the jingle of harness, the blowing of horses that had been ridden hard. The walnut grips of the Colt felt reassuring under his fingers.

Three men appeared in the doorway, grins on their faces as they chuckled at something said by one of them. They stopped short when they saw the defensive attitude of the men inside.

"Howdy, Donaldson," the one in the lead said to the tavernkeeper. "Looks like you're expectin' trouble."

Donaldson visibly relaxed. "Hell, Brewster, we just didn't know who you was. A man's got to be careful out here, you know that."

"Sure," the one called Brewster replied easily. "We come to see if you got some more of that whiskey."

"Just unloadin' it now." Donaldson lowered his shotgun and said to Benton and Glidinghawk, "You don't have to worry about these boys. They're regular customers o' mine."

Benton nodded and motioned for Glidinghawk to follow him. The strangers moved aside to let them by as they went back out to the wagon.

Glidinghawk studied the three strangers out of the corner of his eye as he went past them. All three were young and dressed in range clothes, none too clean. And they all wore handguns. The one called Brewster wore two pistols in a fancy rig. Cowhands, more than likely, Glidinghawk decided, who liked to think of themselves as *pistoleros*. There were cattle spreads here in the Nations, huge ranches leased to white men by the government. The Indians were supposed to get most of that lease money, but it was doubtful that the tribes ever saw more than a small fraction of it.

Brewster and one of the other men trailed along after Benton and Glidinghawk to watch as they climbed into the wagon bed. The other man lounged near the mule team, while Brewster rested his hands on the sideboard of the wagon.

"Don't I know you, feller?" Brewster asked, frowning slightly at Moody.

"Could be," Benton grunted. "I been plenty of places."

"Texas, maybe?"

"I been there." Benton's tone was unfriendly, but Brewster didn't seem to notice.

"We're from Texas," the young cowboy went on, ignoring the hostility. "Rode for a couple of different spreads down there, come up the trail last summer with a herd. Took them all the way to Dodge City, we did. The boys and me decided to take our time 'bout moseyin' back home. Figure we'll get there just about the right time to catch on with another drive this summer."

Benton and Glidinghawk had hold of the second barrel and were starting to move it toward the back of the wagon.

Brewster stepped away from the wagon suddenly, his hands moving to the guns on his hips. The Colts came up in a blur of motion, and the sound of the hammers being eared back was uncommonly loud in the night stillness.

"Y'all just leave that barrel right there," Brewster commanded sharply. "That'll save us havin' to load it up again."

"What the hell?" Benton demanded. "You gone crazy, mister?"

Glidinghawk had frozen as soon as he saw Brewster going for his guns. He glanced at the other man, saw that he had drawn his weapon, too. The two cowboys had the drop on them, all right.

"Nope, we ain't crazy," Brewster said mockingly. "But we know a place we can sell this rotgut and make enough money so that we won't have to eat cow dust all summer long again. We can sit in the shade and pat fancy ladies on the bee-hind. Now you got a choice, fella. You can give up the whiskey peaceful-like, or we can just kill you and take it."

Suddenly, inside the roadhouse, Donaldson's shotgun boomed, followed by three sharp cracks of a handgun. A couple of seconds later, there was a final shot from the pistol.

Brewster's grin widened. "Sounds like Donaldson didn't want to do it peaceful-like. Reckon we might as well shoot you boys, too."

CHAPTER NINE

Glidinghawk moved fast. One hand thumped into Benton Moody's back, shoving the whiskey runner hard to the side. Glidinghawk went the other way, diving over the sideboard of the wagon. He landed hard on the ground, sending stabs of pain through his shoulder, but he ignored them as he rolled and clawed at his gun.

He came up on his knees as he lifted the Colt. A rattle of gunfire came from the other side of the wagon. Glidinghawk saw movement out of the corner of his eye, and jerked his head in that direction as the second cowboy came running around the front of the team.

Flame lanced from the muzzle of the gun in the man's hand. Glidinghawk heard the flat, slapping noise of a slug passing close by his head. He let himself fall over backward as if hit, drawing the gunman closer.

Lying on his back, Glidinghawk raised his pistol and triggered twice.

The gun blasted and bucked against his palm, the roar of the black powder all but deafening him. Through the smoke and shadows, he saw the cowboy stop short, as if he had run into a wall. The man's feet went out from under him and he fell, dropping his gun.

Glidinghawk rolled and came up on his feet again, sure that both of his shots had gone home. The cowboy's legs thrashed for a couple of seconds, then he was still.

Glidinghawk spun, eyes peering intently into the darkness for Benton Moody or the thieving cowhand called Brewster. Silence seemed to have fallen over the roadhouse and the area around it.

A moan came from the ground at the rear of the wagon.

Glidinghawk crouched and slid in that direction. The moonlight cast heavy shadows under the wagon, but the Omaha thought he could see a sprawled shape there. Benton—or the murderous Brewster?

Moving closer, Glidinghawk knelt beside the wounded man. Whoever it was, he wasn't moving much. Glidinghawk put his free hand out and touched the man's shirt. His fingers came away wet and sticky.

A shot rang out from the doorway of the roadhouse, the slug whining off the iron wheel of the wagon close beside Glidinghawk. He whirled away from the wounded man, crawling up toward the mule team. The animals were somewhat skittish from the firing, but they hadn't panicked yet.

"Hold your fire!" Glidinghawk called toward the tavern. "There's no need for us to keep shooting at each other."

"That you, redskin?" Brewster shouted back.

"Yes."

"You don't talk much like an Injun. What do you

87

reckon we ought to do?"

Glidinghawk took a deep breath. "I just started working for these people tonight. I don't want to catch a bullet because of them."

"You're sayin' you'll let me have the whiskey?"

"I can't do that," Glidinghawk said flatly. "But I'll let you ride away from here without any more gunfire."

There was a moment of hesitation while Brewster thought over the offer. "What happened to Gooch?"

"He's the other one who was out here?"

"That's right."

"He came at me firing his gun. I had to kill him."

A humorless chuckle came from the building. "Well hell, that was pretty stupid of him, weren't it? Still, Gooch was my pard, Injun, and I don't reckon I can let you get away with killin' him."

Glidinghawk suddenly heard the crunch of wet sand under boots and realized that Brewster had been stringing him along while the third man slipped out of the roadhouse and tried to get behind him. He whipped around as the man ran to the back of the wagon, firing as fast as he could jerk the trigger.

Glidinghawk dove forward, landing in a puddle. Mud splashed up in his eyes. He blinked rapidly and squeezed off a shot, knowing he had little chance of hitting the man. Within instants, he realized, he was going to be dead.

The heavy boom of a Sharps rumbled through the night like the thunder of the earlier storm. Glidinghawk saw the head of the man who was charging him all but explode from the impact of the heavy ball. The man flopped bonelessly to the ground.

Glidinghawk didn't have time to wonder where the

shot had come from. Brewster was boiling out of the roadhouse door, screaming his rage and pumping bullets at the Omaha. Glidinghawk rolled under the wagon and threw a wild shot at him, missing badly.

Brewster planted his feet and stood his ground, angling both pistol barrels toward Glidinghawk, ready to blow him to shreds.

Behind the kill-crazed cowboy, a bloody shape suddenly lurched out of the building, casting a monstrous shadow in the light that spilled through the door. Donaldson had obviously taken a couple of slugs in the body, but somehow he was still alive—and the shotgun was in his hands.

He had fired only one barrel earlier, Glidinghawk realized. The tavernkeeper staggered up behind Brewster, who was oblivious to the new threat. Donaldson rammed the muzzle of the Greener against the cowboy's spine and fired.

Brewster's body muffled the blast. He shrieked and arched his back, thrown forward by the load of buckshot ripping a massive hole through him. He was dead when he landed facedown in the mud.

Glidinghawk stayed where he was under the wagon, shudders running through him. He was cold. A couple of feet away, Benton Moody moaned again.

Donaldson sat down heavily, the shotgun slipping from his hands. He stayed there, shirt blood-soaked, swaying slightly.

Glidinghawk heard horses coming up to the roadhouse. The hoofbeats stopped, and then booted feet approached. Glidinghawk tightened his grip on the Colt, unsure what was going to happen next.

"You might as well come out from under there,

Injun," Arlie Moody's rough voice growled. "Looks like it's all over."

Benton Moody had caught a slug in the shoulder, the bullet passing on through. Glidinghawk examined him and decided that the bone was chipped but not shattered. Benton was still going to be laid up for a while, though. But barring infection, he would live.

Glidinghawk poured whiskey from one of the barrels over the wound to disinfect it. Benton screamed and tried to writhe in pain, but Arlie and Dirk Moody held their brother down. Glidinghawk bound up the injury, then gave Benton some of the whiskey to drink. He gulped the fiery liquor gratefully, his eyes gradually glazing over as the pain subsided.

Donaldson was more seriously wounded. He had been shot twice in the body, one bullet low on the right side, the other high on the left. He lay on the bar while Glidinghawk worked over him. The tavernkeeper's breath wheezed and whistled in his throat. The squaw stood beside him and held his big-knuckled left hand. It was probably the most blatant show of affection she had ever demonstrated.

"Never expected that boy to pull a gun on me," Donaldson said, gasping for air. Glidinghawk had warned him to be quiet, but evidently he felt the need to explain what had happened. Arlie and Dirk stood close by, listening.

Donaldson continued, "I still got a shot off first—one barrel, anyway. Didn't . . . didn't hit him, though. He got me in the side, knocked me down. B-Bastard come walkin' over with a big grin on his face. . . . Should've put a bullet in my head, but I reckon he went for my heart instead."

Dirk Moody said, "Hell, that was a stupid move. Didn't he know you ain't got a heart, Donaldson?"

"Shut up, Dirk," Arlie growled.

"The bullet hit one of your ribs and deflected off," Glidinghawk said as he cleaned the wounds. "You're a lucky man to come out of this with only a broken rib, some torn-up muscles, and a lot of blood lost."

"Yeah," Donaldson said. "Lucky."

After a moment, he went on, "I laid there, sort of passed out for a few minutes, till I got enough strength back to get outside and blast Brewster."

"I appreciate that," Glidinghawk said. "He would have gone for me."

"Yeah . . . I don't much like havin' an Injun doctorin' me."

"I'll turn the job over to Arlie," Glidinghawk offered.

Arlie held his hands up. "The hell you will. I just shoot 'em, I don't patch 'em up."

"Like that thief outside."

Arlie grinned savagely. "Looked like you needed a mite of help, Glidinghawk."

Finished with Donaldson, the Omaha turned toward Arlie and said flatly, "You followed us. You weren't trusting me with a damned thing."

"Hell, I never even seen you before tonight, boy. You think I'm goin' to let you ride off with four barrels of good rotgut—and my brother?"

"So tonight was a test of sorts," Glidinghawk mused.

"I reckon you could say that."

"And did I pass?"

Arlie grinned again. "You protected my whiskey, killed one of them sidewinders that was tryin' to steal it, and doctored my little brother. Reckon I'm satisfied. But I'll still have my eye on you, mister. You try anything funny and I'll blow you clear to that there happy huntin' ground of yours."

"That's one Indian myth I never believed in," Glidinghawk said grimly. "Let's get this man in a bed. With any luck, he'll be all right, too."

The squaw suddenly spoke for the first time. Glidinghawk didn't understand her language, but he knew she was thanking him. He smiled slightly and nodded to her.

Arlie and Dirk carried Donaldson to his cot behind the hanging blanket. The squaw went with them. There was a brief murmur of conversation. When they emerged, Arlie said, "We'd best be gettin' the rest of that liquor unloaded. Donaldson's squaw'll run the place till he's back on his feet." He went behind the bar and opened a cigar box he found there, taking out a wad of money. "Here's our pay, just like Donaldson said."

Glidinghawk and Dirk rolled the two remaining barrels of whiskey off the wagon and brought them into the roadhouse. That done, they carried Benton out of the building and placed him in the wagon bed, moving him as gently as possible. The wounded man had consumed enough of the whiskey so that he was only semiconscious now, feeling little if any pain.

"Can you handle a mule team?" Arlie asked Glidinghawk.

The Omaha nodded.

"Then tie your hoss on the back of the wagon and get them beasts started south." Arlie swung up into his saddle. "We're goin' home."

Glidinghawk had been right. It was a long ride back to Texas.

He dozed on the wagon seat as he drove through the night. It had been a hell of a day. So much had happened—the fight with Fox, the escape from the stockade, the gun battle at the roadhouse. It seemed like too much to have been packed all into one day. But that was the way life was, he reflected. Too much going on or too little.

They kept moving all night, Arlie allowing a brief stop at dawn for coffee, bacon, and biscuits. Then it was back on the trail.

Benton Moody woke up from his whiskey-induced slumber and began whimpering in pain. Arlie called a halt long enough for Dirk to climb into the back of the wagon and tip another bottle to Benton's mouth. He sucked greedily from it and settled down in a few minutes.

Glidinghawk wasn't sure how good an idea it was to keep pouring whiskey into the wounded man, but at least it was keeping him still and quiet, giving the injury a chance to heal. At any rate, it was the best they could do. His medical skills were limited, and he had no supplies to work with.

They reached the Red River a little after midday. The stream was muddy and shallow and narrow in this region, flowing through a broad valley with slopes so gentle it was hard to distinguish where they began. The terrain was flat and desolate, dotted with tumbleweeds and scrub mesquite. There was a little more vegetation as they approached the river. Everything had a rusty tinge to it, owing to the red clay of the ground.

All in all, it was about as unprepossessing a country as Glidinghawk had ever seen. It became even less impressive as they crossed the river and drove deeper into Texas. The ground was rougher. Hills, bluffs, and miniatures canyons appeared. Dwarf cedars maintained a harsh existence on some of the rocky outcroppings. This was the area known as the Copper Brakes, Glidinghawk knew, where Amos Powell suspected that the whiskey runners had their headquarters.

It looked as if the colonel was right.

As dusk was dropping, the little group topped a rise and started down into a small valley. The approach was not too rough on this side, but the rest of the valley was surrounded by rugged bluffs that would make entering it difficult. Glidinghawk saw a small cleft in the bluff on the opposite side of the valley. Perhaps there was another exit through that winding gully, but if so, it would be easily defended.

It came as no surprise to him that there was a cabin in the center of the valley, a thin plume of smoke drifting from its chimney. Behind the cabin was another building, a little smaller, with its own chimney. Smoke came from it, too.

Arlie Moody pulled his horse to a stop and pointed with a blunt finger. "There she be," he said to Glidinghawk. "Home."

Glidinghawk watched through the gathering shadows as two figures came onto the porch of the cabin. Both were women—he could tell that from the long skirts they wore—but other than that he couldn't say anything about them.

Arlie lifted his rifle and waved it above his head.

One of the female figures returned the gesture. "All clear," Arlie grunted. "Let's go, boys."

Glidinghawk flapped the reins and started the mules moving again. As the wagon bounced down the hill, he realized that he had accomplished one more objective. He was willing to bet that the smaller building contained a still where the whiskey was produced.

He wondered in that moment where Landrum and Celia were. They were supposed to be working on the same problem from the other end. Had they had any luck?

No matter, he decided. For now, the outcome of this mission appeared to be up to him.

CHAPTER TEN

"I'm getting bored, Landrum," Celia Louise Burnett said, a dangerous edge in her voice.

Keeping his voice low-pitched, Landrum replied, "You're not the only one, dammit. What do you want me to do—start asking people on the street if they know who's cooking whiskey and then smuggling it into the Indian Territory?"

"Hush," Celia hissed. "You know that's not what I want. I just wish something would happen."

They were walking down the single main street of Truscott, Texas, heading toward O'Leary's Shamrock Saloon. Lanterns were being lit in the buildings they passed as twilight fell over the small settlement.

They had been in Truscott for a week now, and to their chagrin, they were no closer to locating the whiskey runners than when they had arrived. During that time, they had frequented O'Leary's place and kept their eyes and ears open while trying to leave the impression that they were overly fond of their drink and none too scrupulous.

So far, no one seemed to have paid any attention to them.

Landrum was tired of this routine, and he knew

Celia was, too. Over the next couple of days, he decided, he would ride out from Truscott into the Brakes and have a look around.

They turned in at O'Leary's and were greeted congenially by the white-haired saloonkeeper as they pushed through the batwings. They had become good customers.

O'Leary was pouring their drinks before they reached the bar. Landrum picked up the whiskey and downed it gratefully, letting his eyes wander to the mirror behind the bar so that he could study the Shamrock's occupants.

The place was fairly busy tonight. Being the only place in town to drink, O'Leary's did a steady business. There were at least half a dozen cowboys from the nearby ranches, a couple of townsmen, and the gambler, whose name was Garrick.

Landrum had gotten to know the man fairly well and had even shared a few hands of poker with him. As they played, he saw why Garrick was content to stay in Truscott, even though the pickings had to be pretty slim around here for a professional gambler. Simply put, he wasn't very good at it. But he was friendly enough, and careful about his cheating. He never tried anything when he was dealing to Landrum, and he made a point of never nicking anyone for very much.

Tonight, Garrick hailed Landrum from his usual table and said, "Join us in a game of chance, Mr. Davis?" There were two cowhands sitting at the table with Garrick. The gambler idly shuffled the deck of cards in his slender hands.

Landrum glanced at Celia. "Go ahead," she

shrugged. She sipped from the glass of whiskey in her hand. "I'll stay here and talk to Mr. O'Leary."

Landrum nodded and went over to the table, pulling back a chair and sitting down as he greeted the other players.

Celia finished her drink and pushed the empty glass across the bar to O'Leary. "Another, darlin'?" he asked her.

"Another," Celia agreed. She tried to keep the morose tones out of her voice but wasn't very successful.

O'Leary splashed liquor into the glass and looked shrewdly at Celia. "Somethin's troubling ye, lass. Is there anything I can do?"

"Oh, no, I'm fine," Celia insisted. She drank a little more.

Taking a deep breath, she became aware that O'Leary was glancing down at the thrust of her breasts in the low-cut gown. The old goat, she thought. But at least he was a fairly nice old goat.

"Garrick was askin' me earlier why you don't ever join their games. The lad seems to admire you."

Celia shook her head. "Poker's not really my game. I like playing occasionally, but I prefer faro."

"Like to buck the tiger, eh? Well, I'm afraid ye'll not find many faro players around here. These local lads are a simple sort. They like their poker and beer, but their tastes are not what you'd call sophisticated."

Celia stared at the glittering array of bottles on the back bar, barely listening to the old man. Her mind had drifted back a couple of years to Fort Griffin, Texas, far south of here, where Powell's Army had been assigned to their first mission. The denizens of the area known as the Flats—a rabbit's warren of bordellos and gambling houses—had not been sophisticated either. And yet among them she had met the man called Black Jack. He had taught her a great deal about life—and love. She had lost her innocence with him, given it up freely.

And then he had been horribly murdered.

A shiver ran through her as the memories replayed themselves in her mind. After that mission, it had been a long time before she had allowed herself to feel anything deeply for a man. Then, on the way to Denver for their most recent assignment, she had met Major Devlin Henry.

Devlin had still been alive when Powell's Army left Denver, their mission brought o a successful conclusion with his assistance. But he had gone his way and Celia had gone hers. She could have resigned from the team, she knew; she was a civilian, after all, and Amos Powell had no real hold on her. She had decided against it, though, decided to remain a part of the group. She was not ready to settle down.

But that didn't mean she couldn't regret the decision from time to time—like now. The domestic life could not have been any more boring than the week they had spent in Truscott.

Over at the table, Landrum was having mixed luck. He was winning a little more than he was losing, and he was content with that for the moment. The two cowhands were strangers, and he learned from casual conversation with them that they worked on a spread northwest of Truscott, on the edge of the Copper Brakes.

"Pretty lonely country out there, I imagine," Landrum commented idly as he studied his cards.

"Damn right," one of the men agreed. "You can ride all day and not see another soul."

"Anybody live out there in the Brakes?"

"A few old hermits," the other cowboy answered. "And a few idiots who try to farm or ranch on that damned clay. It won't raise a crop, and there ain't enough graze for more than a couple of head in ten miles. The spread we ride for is about like the end of the world, mister. Nothin' between there and the Red River."

"What about the Moodys?" the first cowboy asked. "You forgettin' about them?"

"Hah! Reckon they're hermits and idiots. Never seen an unfriendlier bunch, or a crazier one."

"I wouldn't let any of them hear you say that," Garrick warned solemnly. "You know how violent the whole lot of them can be."

"Moody . . ." Landrum mused. "Wasn't that the name of the fellow who nearly caused a fight the day Miss Burnett and I arrived?"

Garrick nodded. "I believe you're right. That was Claude Moody. He's got three brothers, all of them just as touchy. One of them was with him that day, but I don't remember which one."

"Their ma's the craziest one of the bunch," one of the cowhands said. "Only seen her once, when they all come to town for supplies. She was quotin' the Bible one minute, then cussin' a blue streak and takin' a quirt after them boys the next. I ain't surprised they're all teched in the head, bein' raised by that she-wolf."

The other puncher grunted and said, "Are we here to play cards or talk about them damned Moodys?"

"I'm playing cards," Landrum said with a grin, lay-

100

ing down his hand. The others looked at it, sighed, and threw in their cards as he raked the pot over in front of him.

The wheels of his brain were clicking over rapidly. He had been playing cards, and drinking, and engaging in idle conversations like this one for a damned week now, with a single lack of success. Now all of his instincts were telling him that he had finally stumbled over something. The Moody family certainly sounded like the type who would be involved with something like whiskey smuggling.

And if they lived far out in the Brakes, as the cowboys had indicated, they would be in a good spot to produce the stuff that was being run over the border into Indian Territory.

Of course, the Moodys might be completely harmless. He had absolutely no evidence to support the theory that had suggested itself to him.

But there was nothing disproving it either.

While Landrum was shuffling the cards, one of the cowboys leaned back in his chair and began to roll a quirly. As he lit it, he said, "Speakin' of the Moodys, I've heard tell that all them boys have squaws." Disapproval was evident in his voice.

"Hell, what's wrong with that?" the other puncher spoke up. "A woman's a woman, the way I see it. Anyway, that might explain why they ain't afraid of the raidin' parties that come down from the Nations."

Landrum started to deal. "Is there much Indian trouble around here these days?" he asked, willing to push the conversation a little farther since someone else had brought up the subject again.

"Things have been quiet for the last couple of

weeks," Garrick answered. "But before that, raids were pretty common. Small bands would come down from the reservations on the other side of the Red River and rustle cattle, steal horses, things like that. They even pulled some holdups and stole money."

Landrum frowned. "Indians stealing money? That doesn't sound right."

"Maybe not," Garrick shrugged. "But it's true."

"We've had to run them red devils off from the ranch a couple of times," one of the men added. "Even then, they made off with some beeves." The puncher shook his head. "It's a downright shame, the way them savages sit up there on the reservation, pretendin' to be so civilized, and all the time they're plannin' their raids down here."

"When did all this trouble start?" Landrum asked.

"Been goin' on for months now."

In other words, ever since the whiskey traffic into the Nations had picked up, Landrum thought. It was all tying in.

He played a couple more hands, losing them both, and then decided to call it a night. He wanted to get back to Celia and tell her what he had discovered. If she agreed with him that the Moodys sounded like good suspects, he would have a starting place for the rest of their investigation.

"I believe I'll say good night, gentlemen," he said, gathering up his winnings. They totaled a little less than ten dollars, he saw. Still, that was better than losing ten bucks.

"Say, mister," one of the cowboys said in a low voice as Landrum started to stand up. "I know that lady over at the bar is with you, but did I hear you call her *Miss*

Burnett?"

"That's right," Landrum replied. "She's my friend, but we're not married."

"In that case, you reckon she'd object to havin' a dance with me? I can get old O'Leary to unlimber his fiddle and play a tune or two."

Landrum paused, unsure how to answer, not wanting to answer for Celia. Truscott was notably low on women, especially single women. There was one whorehouse, if a shanty shared by two soiled doves could be called such. Every time he and Celia came into the Shamrock, the men there eyed her with undisguised lust, and this evening had been no different. That was one reason he had been able to win at cards—the cowboys were too busy stealing glances at Celia to properly study their hands.

Finally, he said, "I can't speak for the lady. You'll have to ask her yourself, friend."

The cowboy stood up, as did his companion. Both young men suddenly looked nervous. The second one said, "If you're askin' her to dance, so am I."

"Hell, I thought of it first."

"Don't give a damn. I'm askin' her."

A grin twitched the corners of Landrum's mouth. He was sure Celia would adore having two such gallant, dashing young men at odds over her, he thought sarcastically. Just as sure as he was that the two cowhands had had at least one bath each during the last year.

Bumping shoulders in their haste to get to the bar first, the two punchers came up to Celia and at the same time said, "Ma'am?"

She turned, saw them standing there in filthy range

clothes, looked past them, and saw that sly look on Landrum's face. Damn him, she thought tiredly. What had he gotten her into now?

"Ma'am, I'd be right pleased if you'd do me the honor of dancin' with me," one of the cowboys said hurriedly, running the words together in his haste to get the question out before his friend could ask her the same thing.

The other one slapped him on the shoulder with the battered Stetson he held in his hands. "Durn it, I was goin' to ask her first!" he protested. "It was my idea!"

Again, Celia glanced at Landrum. He had stopped smiling now, she saw, and as their eyes met, he gave her a minuscule nod. For some reason, he wanted her to go along with their requests and give them a dance.

Carefully composing her face into a pleasant expression, she said, "Now, boys, there's no need to fight. I'll be happy to dance with both of you."

For a moment, they didn't seem to comprehend that she had accepted, then both of them exclaimed together, "Me first!"

Celia held up her hands. "No arguing, I said. A gentleman always leaves such choices to the lady in question." Arbitrarily, she extended a hand to the puncher on her right. "And I choose you."

The cowboy's face lit up as he took her hand in his grimy, calloused fingers. His partner looked distinctly displeased.

Celia's choice looked at O'Leary and said excitedly, "Break out that fiddle of yours, mister. Play us a jig."

"All right," O'Leary nodded, reaching under the mahogany and coming up with an instrument whose wood was polished to a sheen that matched that of the bar. He had a bow with it, and he quickly plucked out a few notes, tuning the fiddle as he did so.

Then he launched into a merry tune, and before Celia knew what was happening, the cowboy had his arms around her and they were whirling around the small open space between the bar and the tables.

The other customers began to clap their hands, keeping time with the fiddle and getting into the spirit of things. Even the second cowboy got over his anger and started to clap. Celia caught a glimpse of Landrum joining in, an open grin on his face now.

They had been dancing for a couple of minutes when the batwings banged open. O'Leary stopped his playing abruptly, and sobs of pain filled in the sudden silence. Two men staggered into the saloon, one of them supporting the other.

The second man had no face.

CHAPTER ELEVEN

On second shocked glance, the injured man did have a face. It was just the features were obscured by the torrent of blood that had cascaded down over them. His entire head was a crimson ruin.

He had been scalped—and he was still alive.

"Help us!" the youth holding him up shrieked. "Pa's hurt! Help him!" The boy was perhaps seventeen, and his own shirt was soaked with blood. It was impossible to tell if he was wounded or if the gore had come from his father's hideous injury.

Suddenly, the young man began to sag, obviously drained. Landrum was the only one in the saloon with the presence of mind to react in time. He sprang forward, his steely grip fastening on the boy's arm and holding him up. Together, he and the boy lowered the older man to the floor.

Landrum looked up at O'Leary. "Is there a doctor around here?" he rapped.

The Irishman shook his head. "Hughie the barber is as close as we've got to a doctor." O'Leary glanced at one of the cowhands. "Ted! Go fetch him!"

The puncher nodded and left the saloon at a run.

Celia was staring in horrified fascination at the

wounded man. She had seen violent death many times, but this was one of the worst things she had ever witnessed. The scalped man was breathing hoarsely and raggedly. His eyes were closed, and his fingers twitched uncontrollably as he lay on the sawdust-covered floor. Landrum had sunk down beside him and had the man's head supported on his leg, ignoring the blood that was soaking his pants.

Garrick and O'Leary joined him, kneeling on either side of the wounded man. Garrick put his hands on the shoulders of the boy, who was on his knees, heaving deep breaths into tortured lungs. "Are you all right, son?" Garrick asked. "Are you wounded, too?"

The boy shook his head. "No-no . . . I'm all right. It's Pa. . . . The damned Injuns come raidin' the farm, tried to run off our cows. . . . Pa started shootin' at 'em"—he buried his face in his hands and let out a huge sob—"an' then they shot him and did that to him! took his hair, goddamn them!"

Celia shuddered. She realized that the cowboy still had his arm around her and that she was leaning against his dirt-encrusted vest. At the moment, she didn't care. After seeing what had come stumbling into the saloon, she was just glad to have another human being close by to hold her.

"They rode off when they was through with him," the boy went on when his sobs had subsided. "I wanted to fight them, but Pa was still . . . was still awake somehow. He told me to let 'em go, that he didn't want me gettin' killed. I picked him up and started toward town with him. The redskins took all our horses, too."

"That's the Huddleston boy," the cowboy holding Celia told her in a low voice. "Him and his daddy have a farm a couple miles east of here."

"Just them?" Celia asked. "No women?"

The cowboy shook his head. "No women, thank the Lord." His youthful face was grim as he went on, "Looks like the Injun trouble is startin' up again, right enough."

That was an understatement, Celia thought, shuddering again.

A few minutes later, the cowboy who had been sent to get the barber burst through the batwings, a portly figure following closely behind him. "What the hell happened?" the stout man asked.

"Ab Huddleston got himself scalped by a bunch of heathens," O'Leary replied. "Do what ye can for him, Hughie."

The barber nodded and stripped off his coat, tossing it on the bar. He began to roll up his sleeves as he knelt beside the wounded man. "Hot water and whiskey," he snapped. "And plenty of cloths, as clean as you can find them."

The cowboy holding Celia gently turned her toward the bar, so that she wouldn't see what was happening as Hughie began his work. Celia didn't resist. Watching was the last thing she wanted to do.

"I could use a drink," she said softly.

"You and me both," the cowboy agreed. He leaned over the bar and reached under it to pull out a bottle. "Don't reckon O'Leary will mind folks helpin' themselves, under the circumstances."

The second cowboy, who had been vying for Celia's attention, joined them and said, "Pour me a slug of that, too." He slapped a coin on the bar to cover the drinks.

Celia took the glass offered her and sipped the liquor, taking comfort from the embers it kindled in her belly. She kept her eyes on the mahogany. She could avoid the sight of what had happened, she realized, but she couldn't shut out the sobs of the boy or the desperate gasping breaths of the father.

Everyone in the saloon heard the death rattle.

Celia closed her eyes and leaned against the bar, her fingers tightening on the glass in her hand. "I'm sorry," she heard Hughie the barber murmur. "There just wasn't a damned thing I could do to save him. He'd lost too much blood."

"Aye," O'Leary said.

"You did your best," Garrick added. "Come on, boys, let's get him down to the undertakers."

Hughie said, "Vern, you come with me. Ain't anything you can do for your pa now."

Celia looked up and saw the image in the mirror as O'Leary pressed a full bottle into Hughie's hand. "The boy needs sleep," the saloonkeeper said softly. "Use as much of this as you have to."

Hughie nodded, then with his arm around the youth's shoulders to help hold him up, he left the Shamrock.

Landrum came up to the bar a moment later, looking down at the massive bloodstain on his pants and shaking his head. "Awful business," he said. His face was bleak.

"Aye, that it is," O'Leary agreed as he went behind the bar again.

"Is this the kind of thing that's been happening around here?"

Garrick joined the little group and answered Landrum's question. "It's usually not this bad, but this isn't the first time the Indians have killed on one of their raids. There have probably been half a dozen instances of folks fighting back and getting a bullet or an arrow for their trouble. This is the first scalping that I know of, though."

"Can't the army or the Texas Rangers do anything?" Landrum knew the answer to that question even as he asked it. The army was overextended owing to Indian troubles farther west, and the Rangers had historically been too few in number to deal with such problems except on a limited basis. A few years earlier, Landrum had been a Ranger himself, and even though he was convinced they were the best group of fighting men the world had ever seen, there just weren't enough of them.

Garrick shrugged. "The army and the Rangers try. But the way those braves come down out of the Nations and then run back there when they're through, it's hard to track them down and prove anything."

Landrum tossed back the drink that O'Leary had poured for him and tried to look resigned. "Well, I guess it's none of my business anyway. There's always going to be trouble out here. Folks know that when they come."

O'Leary frowned at him. "A bit of a callous attitude, don't ye think?"

"Life's been hard on all of us, not just those poor settlers," Landrum said coldly.

Celia hoped none of the others gave much thought to how Landrum's words contrasted with his earlier actions. He had been the first to try to help the Huddlestons and had stayed right with them until Ab Huddleston's death. That behavior didn't jibe very well with the coldhearted image Landrum was now trying to project.

Instinct sometimes made a man act without thinking. That was what Landrum had done when he'd seen someone in trouble.

And whether or not that clashed with his cover identity, Celia had to respect him for it.

It might be best if they left, Celia thought. She said, "Landrum, darling, if you don't mind I'd like to go home. I'm not feeling too well."

"Of course," he said quickly. "I can understand that. All this was too much for you."

"Y-Yes," she said picking up on what he wanted from her. "I feel a bit faint."

He took her arm with a strong hand and turned toward the door, tossing a coin to O'Leary to pay for their drinks. Garrick and the two cowboys seemed sorry to see them, go, but Landrum bid them farewell and steered Celia to the door. She sagged slightly against him, as if overcome with emotion. Actually, that wasn't far from the truth.

As they went out, Landrum said in a voice loud

enough for the men at the bar to hear, "I want to get these pants changed. All that blood! They're probably ruined."

They turned down the rough sidewalk toward the Stanley house, and Celia hissed, "God, that was awful, Landrum!"

"It sure as hell was," he agreed quietly. "I found out something during that poker game, though, before that poor bastard and his boy came in."

"You mean you've turned up a lead to the whiskey runners?"

"Maybe." Quickly, Landrum filled her in on what he had learned about the mysterious Moody family. When he was done, she agreed that they sounded like the kind of clan that would be involved in something illegal.

"But how are you going to locate them?" she asked.

"I'm going to work on O'Leary a little more. He has to have some sort of liquor supply he can buy in an emergency. He has most of his whiskey freighted in, but there are bound to be times when he runs short and can't get any more here for several days."

"You think he might buy liquor from the Moodys when that happens?"

"If the Moodys are even involved in the whiskey production," Landrum reminded her. "But I think it's worth investigating."

"I agree," Celia said, nodding her red head. "We have to do whatever we can to stop them, Landrum. We have to get rid of the reason for those Indian raids, like the one tonight—"

She broke off, a shiver making her tremble. Landrum felt it through the arm he had around her shoulder.

"We'll find them," he promised in a soft but dangerous voice. "And we'll stop them."

CHAPTER TWELVE

Gerald Glidinghawk was right about the two figures who appeared on the porch of the cabin being female, but he was not prepared for what he found when the wagon rolled to a stop in front of the ramshackle building.

The older and taller of the two women stared at him with an intense glare in her faded blue eyes. She was thin and spare, and her braided hair was snow white. She wore a drab cotton dress with a crocheted shawl draped around her shoulders.

One gnarled hand held the barrel of a carbine. The butt of the weapon rested on the planks of the porch, and it was almost unnoticeable as it leaned against the folds of her dress.

Arlie Moody swung down from his horse and looped the reins over a hitch rail in front of the cabin. "Howdy, Ma," he said.

"A heathen!" the old woman spat at him. "You brought a godless, bloody-handed heathen to our home, boy! The Good Lord will smite you for that, you no-good stupid bastard."

"Aw, hell, Ma, Glidinghawk's no heathen. He's workin' for us now, and he's already helped save a load

114

of whiskey from a bunch of skunks who was tryin' to steal it."

From the back of the wagon, Benton Moody let out a groan. He tried to lift his head as he quavered, "M-Ma? Is that you, Ma . . . ?"

The old woman's eyes widened, losing some of the fanatical light that burned in them. "Benton?" she asked softly. "Benton, are you all right, boy?"

"He's been shot," Arlie said heavily. "Come on, Dirk, help me get him inside."

"Shot!" Ma Moody shrilled. She rushed down the steps from the porch. "Get out of my way!" she snarled at Dirk.

Glidinghawk glanced over his shoulder as the old woman scrambled spryly into the back of the wagon and took Benton's head in her lap. The Omaha paid little attention to her words as she began to fuss over her wounded son. He was looking at the other woman who still stood on the porch.

She wore a cotton dress like the old woman, but she would have been more at home in buckskins, Glidinghawk thought. Her skin had a rich red hue, made more pronounced by the glare of the setting sun. Her high cheekbones and her long, lustrous raven hair were proof positive of her heritage.

She was as lovely a woman as Glidinghawk had seen in a long time.

She didn't meet his eyes as he gazed at her, and too late, Glidinghawk realized that he was staring. Arlie Moody snapped peevishly, "Dammit, Glidinghawk, quit your gawkin' and get them mules unhitched!"

Glidinghawk pulled his eyes away from the shy beauty and hopped down from the wagon seat. Arlie

115

was frowning darkly at him, and Glidinghawk wondered if the squaw was his woman. Arlie looked like a man who had just had his toes stepped on.

Arlie and Dirk finally persuaded their mother to let them unload Benton and carry him into the shack. While they were doing that, Glidinghawk unhitched the mules and led them into a small pole corral a short distance away from the buildings. There was a water trough there, and a little grass for grazing.

When he returned to the cabin, there was no one outside. However, he could hear the shrill voice of the old woman inside as she harangued her sons. ". . . damned foolishness!" Glidinghawk heard. "Hiring that redskin and then letting your brother get shot like that!"

Glidinghawk stepped up onto the porch as Arlie protested, "I told you, Ma, we didn't *let* Benton get shot. How the hell was we supposed to know them cowboys would try to steal the whiskey? 'Sides, if'n Glidinghawk hadn't been there, Benton probably would've got hisself killed for sure, instead of just shot up a little."

A smile tugged at Glidinghawk's face. There was a whining tone in Arlie's voice, even as he defended their actions. To the rest of the world, he might be a hardened desperado, but facing the wrath of his hag of a mother, the part of him that was still a small boy began struggling to get out.

The door was open a few inches. Glidinghawk put his hand on it and started to push it back.

The Indian woman appeared, grasping the edge of the door to stop it and sliding out through the narrow opening. "Not come in now," she said quietly in English. "Not good idea."

She was either Cheyenne or Sioux—Glidinghawk wasn't sure which. He moved back to let her come onto the porch and pull the door shut behind her.

"I'm not sure it's a good idea for you to be out here, either," he said. "Arlie didn't seem to like me even looking at you. He's not going to care for us being alone out here."

She laughed shortly, humorlessly. "Not worry about husband. Sun Woman make him happy, he forget about Indian brave."

"That's your name? Sun Woman?"

"That is how I am called."

Glidinghawk went to the railing around the porch and carefully leaned on it. The structure didn't look as if it would support a great deal of weight. "How's Benton?" he asked.

"Benton be all right, I think. Need rest most of all."

Glidinghawk nodded. "I kept a close eye on him during the trip down here from the Nations. He seemed to be doing all right. I think I caught the wound in time to keep it from getting infected."

"You . . . doctor?" Sun Woman asked hesitantly.

"No," Glidinghawk replied with a shake of his head. "But I do know a little about medicine, both the white man's kind and the Indian ways of healing."

She changed the subject by asking, "What Arlie say is true? You work for Moodys?"

"Yes, I do. I'm going to help them deliver their whiskey up to Indian Territory." He looked at Sun Woman shrewdly. "That's where you're from, isn't it?"

She looked away. "Sun Woman live here now," she said stubbornly, not wanting to discuss anything that might have come before. She declared, "All Moodys have squaws. Sun Woman is Arlie's squaw."

"Where are the other women?" Glidinghawk asked. He hadn't seen a sign of anyone else on the place.

"Some inside," Sun Woman said, nodding toward the door of the shack. "Benton's woman cry over him, make Ma mad. Other squaws work at still."

"Out there?" Glidinghawk asked, gesturing toward the smaller building.

"Yes. Whiskey come from there. All work, keep fire going, make sure no problems."

This whiskey business was a family affair all the way around, Glidinghawk realized.

He was already thinking about what he could do to break it up. There was nothing he could accomplish by himself. He would only get a bullet for his trouble if he tried. No, he had to get a message giving the place's location to the army somehow, either through Landrum and Celia in Truscott or through Fox back up at Fort Supply. Truscott was quite a bit closer, but there would be no troops there.

He took a deep breath. "Well, Sun Woman, my name is Glidinghawk. The white man knows me as Gerald Glidinghawk. I was born an Omaha."

"You sound like white man now," she said coolly.

"I lived among them for many years and went to their schools," he explained. "But I am an Indian, and I want to be your friend."

She snorted. "Sun Woman have no friends."

"That's a shame. A woman like you should have many friends."

The door of the cabin opened suddenly, and Arlie Moody strode out onto the porch. His eyes flicked from side to side, noting where Glidinghawk and Sun Woman stood, and the Omaha was glad he had kept a respectable distance between himself and the squaw. He thought he could work on her, maybe get her on his side, but he didn't want to move too fast. That would only frighten Sun Woman and probably make Arlie want to put a slug in him.

"How's your brother?" Glidinghawk asked quickly, to get Arlie's mind off of any suspicions he might have.

"Reckon he'll be all right," Arlie said. "Ma says he will anyway, and Ma usually gets what she wants."

"I'm afraid your mother doesn't like me. Perhaps it would be best if I moved on."

"The hell it would," Arlie grunted. "We needed help to start with, and now with Benton laid up for a while, you're goin' to come in right handy 'round here, mister. Don't you mind Ma's talkin' none. She don't like Injuns, never has since the Comanch' killed our pa. But she won't bother you if you just stay out of her way."

"I'll try to do that," Glidinghawk said dryly.

There was a lantern hanging on a peg beside the door. Arlie picked it up, struck a match, and lit it. The shadows of evening had gathered while Glidinghawk and Sun Woman were talking, and now the lantern gave off a welcome circle of light.

"Come on," Arlie said. "Might as well show you around whilst Ma's fussin' and frettin' over Benton."

Leaving the Indian woman on the porch, Glidinghawk followed Arlie toward the other building. Arlie went on, "Reckon you met Sun Woman back there. She's my squaw, Glidinghawk, and you'd best remember that."

"I have no wish to cause trouble."

"Good," Arlie grunted. "All us boys got squaws from up in Injun Territory. We do a good trade in 'em, and we all like to sample the best 'uns for a while."

"I understand." Glidinghawk kept his voice calm, hiding the seething rage he felt building up inside.

This was rapidly becoming more than just another mission to him. He was developing a genuine hatred for Arlie Moody and the other members of his clan. . . .

The smaller building had no windows. Arlie swung open the door and stepped inside, motioning for Glidinghawk to follow him.

Inside was one large room. To one side was a huge metal drum with a fire under it. This was the boiler, Glidinghawk knew. Coils of copper tubing led from the top of it, winding around to drip into a heavy barrel like the ones Glidinghawk had helped unload up in Indian Territory. This massive still was the source of the illegal liquor that was flooding into the Nations, and from what Sun Woman had said, Glidinghawk guessed that the still was probably kept going nearly all the time.

There were two Indian women standing near the fire, keeping an eye on it. They didn't even glance at Arlie and Glidinghawk as the two men came into the room. Evidently they knew their place quite well.

Neither of these women was as attractive as Sun Woman, but both were fairly young and slim. They would fetch a decent price when the Moody brothers tired of them and decided to sell them as prostitutes or virtual slaves.

"Ever seen such a still before?" Arlie asked, pride in

his voice.

"I don't believe I've ever seen one quite so large," Glidinghawk answered. "How much whiskey can it turn out?"

"More'n enough for them red brethren of yours north of the Red River." Arlie laughed shortly. "We supply the whole damn Territory. When Ma first got the idea of buildin' this still, there was several other fellers in the whiskey business up in the Nations. All of 'em have retired permanent-like now."

Glidinghawk knew what he meant. The Moodys had killed off all the competition. That didn't surprise him. He had never encountered a group that seemed as ruthless as this frontier family.

Arlie quickly explained the operation of the still, although Glidinghawk was already familiar with the mechanics of the liquor-producing apparatus. He kept quiet while Arlie talked and let his mind wander back to the other cabin.

With Benton Moody laid up, that left three Moody brothers and the old woman to defend the place. Glidinghawk didn't think the squaws would take a hand in any battle. If the army could raid the place, it would probably all be over quickly.

Even he and Landrum might be able to take on the Moodys in an emergency, he thought. The odds would not be good, but it could be done. He sensed that Arlie was the most dangerous of the brothers, even though he had not yet met the fourth brother, Claude. Ma Moody was an enigma. She did not look particularly dangerous, but Glidinghawk had an uneasy feeling that he would not want her skulking around behind his back.

As an afterthought, Arlie introduced the two women working at the still. Glidinghawk snapped his attention back to the present as Arlie said. "This here's Crying Dove and Small Tongue. They b'long to Claude and Dirk. Benton's woman is called Calf Moon. He ain't goin' to be in shape to take care of her for a while; you might get a little lovin' there if you need it."

Glidinghawk smiled, trying to conceal the distaste he felt for the suggestion. "I'll remember that," he said noncommitally.

"Just don't forget what I told you 'bout Sun Woman."

"You have nothing to worry about, Arlie," Glidinghawk assured him. "I know better than to cross you."

"Good," Arlie grunted. "You hungry?"

"I could eat," Glidinghawk admitted.

Arlie jerked his head toward the door. "I'll have Sun Woman rustle us some grub. Come on."

Again Glidinghawk followed while Arlie carried the lantern. When they reached the porch of the main cabin, Arlie said, "You best wait out here a minute. I'll make sure Ma's busy with Benton. Wouldn't want her takin' her carbine after you."

Glidinghawk smiled thinly. "No, indeed."

Arlie vanished into the house, taking the lantern with him, and Glidinghawk stood on the porch, gazing out at the night. Darkness had fallen completely now, and the stars were brilliant dots high overhead in the clear sky.

It was going to be a pretty night, Glidinghawk thought.

He wasn't sure how long he'd stood there before the door opened again and Sun Woman stepped out onto the porch. She carried a plate of food in her hands, and the smells drifting from it were enough to remind Glidinghawk that he had not eaten since the middle of the day. A long time, and a long way back up the trail.

"Here," Sun Woman said flatly. "You eat."

Glidinghawk took the plate. "Thank you," he said solemnly. "I take it the old lady is still on the warpath, so to speak, when it comes to my presence."

Sun Woman frowned and shook her head. "You talk strange. Ma very angry, if that is what you ask. Better you stay outside tonight."

"All right, but it's liable to get a little chilly before morning," Glidinghawk said around a mouthful of stew that tasted as good as it smelled.

"Sun Woman fix that," she declared. Glidinghawk frowned, unsure what she'd meant, as she disappeared into the house. She came back a moment later and shoved a blanket into his hands. "There!"

Glidinghawk tried not to feel too disappointed.

CHAPTER THIRTEEN

Even with the blanket, Glidinghawk got cold before morning. He slept on the porch, huddled against the wall of the cabin. His slumber was restless, not only because of the uncomfortable bed but because he didn't want Ma Moody sneaking up on him in the night with a butcher knife.

When the sun was turning the sky pink over the bluffs to the east, Glidinghawk stood up and stretched, trying to get the stiffness out of his muscles. There was a well off to one side of the main cabin; he headed for it, intending to wash his face and wake himself up better.

The well was surrounded by a low stone wall. A simple windlass arrangement was built over it on a wooden frame. The bucket attached to the rope was sitting on the stone wall.

Just as Glidinghawk reached the well, the back door of the cabin opened and Sun Woman emerged. She walked toward him carrying a large pan in her hands. Her eyes were downcast, as usual, and she didn't look at him as she came up to the well.

"Good morning," Glidinghawk said softly.

Sun Woman made no reply.

"Come to fetch water?" the Omaha asked, rather stupidly, he thought.

"Sun Woman make coffee, get meal ready," she said. She stood still, obviously waiting for him to get out of her way.

Glidinghawk reached out and took the pan from her before she could protest. He set it on the wall, then grasped the rope and let the bucket down into the well. It was a deep hole, he discovered as he waited for the telltale sound of the bucket hitting the water. When it finally came, he let it fill and then began hauling it back up.

When the nearly full bucket reached the top of the well, Glidinghawk leaned over to grasp its handle and lifted it to pour the rather murky liquid into the pan. He poured out most of the water, leaving a little in the bottom of the bucket. Then he raised it higher and doused his own head. The water was cold, and the sudden shock of it sent a shiver down his spine.

He dropped the bucket down the well again. Another bucketful would fill Sun Woman's pan, he thought.

"You not have to help," she said as he let the rope slide through his palms. "This job squaw's work."

"I don't mind," he said quietly. "I'm glad to help."

He filled his bucket, pulled it back up, and dumped it into the pan. As he had estimated, that filled the vessel. He placed the bucket back on the wall and then reached out to lift the pan.

Sun Woman reached for it at the same time, and their hands touched.

Glidinghawk left his fingers where they were.

Sun Woman glanced toward the main cabin, then

toward the building where the still was located, but she didn't move her hands either. Slowly, her gaze came back to Glidinghawk's face.

"You should not stay here," she said in a voice that was little more than a whisper. "You good man. Sun Woman can tell. These people bad. They hurt you, sooner or later."

"Have they hurt you, Sun Woman?" Glidinghawk's pulse began to speed up as he felt the smooth, warm touch of her fingertips.

She shook her head. "No one hurt Sun Woman," she said fervently. "No one."

Her words were determined, but Glidinghawk thought he saw uncertainty in her eyes. She had been hurt in the past, he suspected, and considering the type of man Arlie Moody was, she was probably still being hurt.

"How in the world did you wind up down here?" he asked, letting his fingers press a little harder against her hands.

Her gaze dropped again. There was shame in her voice as she said, "Sun Woman's husband drank too much of the white man's firewater, died of the sickness it brought. All of Sun Woman's family dead, nowhere to go, no one to hunt for her food. Chief says tribe cannot help, that Sun Woman must leave. Chief gives squaws to Arlie so Arlie gives chief more whiskey." Her slender shoulders lifted and fell in a shrug. "Sun Woman must leave. Nothing else to do."

Glidinghawk grimaced. It was not that unusual a story. There had been a time when every warrior in a tribe would have died rather than let one of the women be forced into such a squalid existence. But those days were dying, killed by the inexorable advance of white civilization across the country.

"This is no way to live," Glidinghawk told Sun Woman. "You are the one who should leave this place."

"Where would Sun Woman go?" she asked bluntly. "Who take care of her?"

Those were questions he couldn't answer.

Given the chance, though, he might be able to help her find the answers for herself.

The creaking of the hinges on the cabin door made Sun Woman jerk back away from him. Some of the water in the pan sloshed over onto Glidinghawk's fingers as he let it go. He looked at the cabin.

Dirk Moody stepped outside, stumbling slightly as he stretched and blinked the sleep out of his eyes. He turned his head toward the well, then started in that direction.

Sun Woman brushed past him, carrying the pan of water. She did not look at him. Dirk frowned slightly at her back, then continued on to the well.

"Mornin', Injun," he said, leaning on the stone wall. "Haul me up some water." The tone of command in his voice was blatant.

"My name is Glidinghawk," the Omaha said stiffly. He longed to pick up the bucket and smash it over Dirk's head.

"Hell, I know that. You're still an Injun, ain't you?"

Glidinghawk said nothing.

"You goin' to get that water for me?" Dirk asked truculently. "Or am I goin' to have to teach you a lesson?"

His face stony, Glidinghawk reached out and picked up the bucket, then began letting it down the well.

As he lowered the bucket, Dirk asked him, "What were you doin' out here with Arlie's squaw?"

"She came to get water," Glidinghawk said simply. "I helped her."

"Why'n the hell would you want to do that?" Dirk sounded genuinely puzzled.

"I was here getting water for myself. It was no problem to do it for her as well." Glidinghawk heard the bucket reach the water at the bottom of the well. He pulled up slightly on the rope to tip the bucket and let it begin to fill.

"Yeah, but if a squaw don't have to do her work, after a while she starts gettin' lazy. Then you got to whomp 'em around some to put the fear o' God back in 'em."

"The fear of your violence, you mean," Glidinghawk said coldly.

Dirk grinned hugely. "Redskin, to them squaws, a white man *is* God. You might ought to remember that."

Glidinghawk hauled the bucket up in silence, then set it on the wall and turned away.

Dirk called after him, "Best stay away from Arlie's woman. He don't like folks messin' with what's his."

"I'll remember that," Glidinghawk said without looking around.

He walked back to the cabin and circled around it, stepping up onto the porch again. As he did so, the front door opened and Ma Moody emerged quickly. There was a shotgun in her hands.

Glidinghawk stopped short, about eight feet from her. Her eyes locked on his face, wide and staring and, at that moment, absolutely insane.

The barrels of the shotgun jerked up toward him.

Glidinghawk's reflexes took over. With an involuntary shout, he threw himself to the side, diving over the porch railing. The shotgun blasted deafeningly, and he heard the buckshot whistling past him. None of the pellets seemed to hit him, though — at least he didn't think so in the split second before he slammed heavily and painfully into the ground.

He scrambled to the side, unsure whether the old woman had fired both barrels or only one. As Glidinghawk glanced over his shoulder at her, he saw that she was tracking him with the gun and that he was not going to be able to get out of range in time.

There was a flicker of movement in the doorway behind Ma Moody, and Arlie was suddenly there, reaching over her shoulder to grasp the barrels of the shotgun. He wrenched upward as she touched off the second shell. The weapon thundered again, but this load of shot pelted into the flimsy roof overhanging the porch. Splinters showered down around Arlie and his crazed mother.

"Ma!" he yelled as he twisted the shotgun out of her grasp. "What the blue blazes are you doin', Ma?"

The old woman lunged with surprising speed toward him, reaching out for the butt of the pistol hanging on his hip. "It's a redskin!" she screeched. "They've come back for the rest of your pa!"

"No, Ma!" Arlie told her urgently. "That's Glidinghawk. He works for us. He's a good Injun, Ma."

From his sprawled position on the ground, Glidinghawk watched in morbid fascination as Arlie held on to his mother and kept her from getting her clawlike fingers on any other weapons. He continued talking, assuring her that Glidinghawk was friendly and no threat. The old woman kept casting wild-eyed glances at the Omaha, but slowly she calmed down and finally let Arlie slip his arm around her shoulders and turn her toward the doorway.

"Sun Woman!" he called sharply.

The Indian woman appeared at the door, and Arlie turned his mother over to her. Sun Woman gently steered Ma Moody into the cabin.

Arlie came down the porch steps, still carrying the shotgun. Glidinghawk had gotten to his feet by now and was brushing some of the clinging red dust from his buckskins.

"Reckon Ma must've spotted you through the window and forgot you wasn't a heathen savage," Arlie said. "She probably figgered you was one of the Comanch', come back to finish the job on Pa."

"Finish the job?" Glidinghawk asked dubiously.

Arlie shrugged his shoulders. "They carved him up pretty good. They must've hacked off a few parts here and there and carried 'em off, 'cause Ma never found all of him. She was by herself, you know. Me 'n' the boys was all off somewheres when the Injuns came. Ma hid under the cabin until they was through with Pa and had rid off. She dug the grave by herself and put him in it." Slowly, Arlie shook his head. "She ain't never been right since then. Might've been better if the redskins had found her, or if they'd burned down the cabin right over her. Would've spared her some pain."

Glidinghawk took a deep breath. He had not been expecting such a story, but the incident that Arlie described was not that unusual on the frontier. There had been instances of incredible violence and brutality on both sides out here. The right and wrong of a thing was hardly an issue anymore—survival was what counted.

"Anyway, I'm sorry Ma let loose at you with that greener," Arlie went on. "That's why I said you'd best keep an eye out and try to steer clear of her."

"I'll be more careful from now on," Glidinghawk promised him.

Arlie's voice hardened. "Dirk says you was out at the well with Sun Woman when he got up. Thought I told you about that last night, Glidinghawk."

"All I did was haul up some water for her," Glidinghawk said wearily. "It was no trouble."

"Dirk thought the two of you was talkin' quite a bit."

Glidinghawk shrugged. "I was just trying to be friendly."

"Well, you can just forget that," Arlie told him icily. "That squaw don't need no friends, especially not some young redskinned buck like you, mister."

For a moment, Glidinghawk's carefully maintained control almost slipped away. He thought fondly of what it would feel like to smash his fist into Arlie's ugly face. But then he said, "I have told you that I will not bother your woman. What else do you want from me?"

"That's all," Arlie said. "That, and do what I tell you when it comes to brewin' and deliverin' that whiskey to the Nations." He jerked his head toward the cabin. "Come on, no hard feelin's. Let's go get us some breakfast."

That sounded better to Glidinghawk than he had expected it to. He fell in beside Arlie Moody and walked toward the cabin, already smelling the intermingled aroma of biscuits, bacon, and coffee that

131

drifted from the shack.

"Any of that buckshot hit you?" Arlie asked.

Glidinghawk shook his head. "I was lucky. She would have hit me with the second barrel if you hadn't stopped her. I appreciate that."

Arlie waved a hand said, "Hell, no thanks necessary. Like I told you, we need you 'round here right now."

"How is your brother Benton this morning?"

"Reckon he's doin' as well as could be expected. He was a mite restless durin' the night, but if we don't run out of whiskey, he'll get the rest he needs. And we ain't likely to be runnin' out!" Arlie laughed.

When they reached the cabin, Arlie told Glidinghawk to wait on the porch for a moment. He disappeared inside, then came back shortly to say, "Ma's layin' down in her room. Reckon it'd be safe enough for you to come in and eat. I don't think she can get her hands on anything to kill you with, even if she does see you."

Glidinghawk didn't feel too reassured by Arlie's words, but he let himself be ushered into the cabin. The smell of breakfast was just too tempting to resist. He remembered that Sun Woman had said she prepared the meals.

He expected the food to be good, and he was right. The bacon was crisp and flavorful, the biscuits light and fluffy. And the coffee, while strong, had a surprisingly good taste.

Glidinghawk sat at a long, roughly hewn table with Arlie, Dirk, and Claude. This was the first time he had met the fourth Moody brother, who had evidently come in late during the night. He was a good match for his brothers, big and brawny, with dark hair and a heavy beard stubble. The family resemblance between all of them was strong.

The Omaha was a bit surprised that they allowed him to eat at the same table with them, but evidently Arlie had laid down the law to Dirk and Claude. Glidinghawk was not to be bothered as long as he stayed in line.

He saw one of the squaws who had been minding the still the night before, and a second one whom he didn't recognize. Claude's woman, no doubt. They served the food, bringing it on big platters from the kitchen where Sun Woman prepared it.

When the meal was over, Arlie scraped his chair back and stood up. "Come on, Glidinghawk," he said, reaching for his hat and taking a Winchester from a rack near the door.

"Where are we going?" Glidinghawk asked.

"You'll be standin' guard some of the time. Figgered you should get the lay of the land."

That made sense. Glidinghawk followed the oldest brother out of the cabin. Arlie nodded toward the corral. "Saddle us up a couple of horses," he said.

Glidinghawk complied, and a few minutes later, the two men rode away from the cabin, heading south. They crossed the rocky flats between the cabin and the bluffs that surrounded it on three sides. Glidinghawk realized that their destination was the narrow canyon cut into the bluff to the south.

"The back door?" he asked, nodding toward the canyon.

"Or the front, dependin' on where you're comin' from," Arlie replied. "The town of Truscott is down that way a few miles. Ever' so often we get folks ridin' out from there. You'll be keepin' an eye on the canyon part of the time, and your job is to watch for anybody who don't belong, who don't have a good reason for bein' out here in the Brakes."

"And if I see someone like that, what do I do?"

Arlie cast a disgusted look over at Glidinghawk as he rode along. "What do you do?" he exclaimed. "Well, what the hell do you think you're supposed to do?" He snorted. "You kill the sons of bitches, that's what you do!"

CHAPTER FOURTEEN

The morning after the scalped man had come stumbling into the Shamrock Saloon, Landrum Davis headed back to O'Leary's. He had a pounding headache, partly from the liquor he had consumed the night before, partly because he hadn't slept well.

Bloody visions had kept haunting his dreams.

Finally, after the third or fourth time he had jerked upright in bed, eyes wide and staring, Landrum had given up. He got up, brewed coffee, and sat at the kitchen table sipping it until Celia came in an hour or so after dawn.

She was yawning, and her red hair was tousled. Landrum thought she was downright beautiful. "Sleep well?" he asked.

"Not particularly," Celia answered with a shake of her head. "I kept dreaming about that poor man."

"Same here."

Celia lifted the coffeepot from the cast iron stove and poured herself a cup. She was wearing a cotton robe, belted tightly around her trim waist. As she carried the coffee to the table and sat down across from Landrum, she said, "I would have thought it wouldn't bother you. You must have seen things that bad and

135

worse a lot of times during the War."

"And afterward, too," Landrum agreed. "When I was with the Rangers, we came on several Indian massacres that were plenty bad. In those days, though, at least we could tell ourselves that the Indians were fighting for what they considered their land, no matter how savagely they did it. Now they're raiding just so that they can get drunk later. It makes a difference."

Celia nodded. "I can see how it would." A shiver ran through her. "What are we going to do now?"

"I'm going to go see O'Leary," Landrum said, standing up and reaching for his hat. "Maybe he can give me a lead on the Moodys."

"What about breakfast?"

Landrum rubbed a hand over his complaining belly. "I don't think I want any," he said. "Not this morning."

Maybe he was just getting old, he thought a few minutes later as he walked down the street. He had never been bothered by a queasy stomach when he was younger, no matter what kind of rotgut and bad food he put in there. And he refused even to consider the possibility that it was the nightmares which had upset him.

He was passing by the First Bank of Truscott when the door of the establishment opened and Randolph Watts stepped out. The banker smiled pleasantly and said, "Good morning, Mr. Davis. How are you enjoying your stay in our fair town?"

Landrum put the best smile he could muster on his face, even though it wasn't much. "Just fine," he said. "It's a right friendly place."

"Small towns usually are," Watts declared proudly.

He was hatless and evidently had just stepped out of the bank for a short constitutional to start the day. He hooked his thumbs in his vest and continued, "I don't mind telling you, I've lived in big cities like Dallas and San Antone, and I wouldn't stay anywhere now but Truscott. No, sir, I sure wouldn't."

The banker was quite adamant, a little too adamant the way Landrum saw it. Truscott was all right, he supposed, but it was hardly the paradise on earth that Watts made it sound like. The surrounding land was rugged and desolate in most directions, even though there were some good ranches in the vicinity, especially to the south and east.

"I guess your bank must be doing all right, from the sounds of it," Landrum commented idly.

Watts nodded. "Yes, indeed. Properly managed, a bank such as this one can be just as lucrative for its officers as one in a larger city. And I am a good manager, sir," he added proudly.

"I'm sure you are," Landrum said, ready to move on and get away from Watts and his chest-thumping. An idea suddenly occurred to him, however, and he said, "I reckon you know most of your depositors, don't you?"

"Of course. That's just part of being a good banker."

"Do some folks called Moody have an account with you? Or isn't that the kind of question a banker can ethically answer?"

Watts frowned. "It's a bit irregular, Mr. Davis, but in this case, I don't mind answering. I know the family you're talking about, and I can assure you they don't have an account in the bank. They're not the sort to trust financial institutions, even if they did have money." The banker hesitated, then asked, "If you don't mind a question, why do you want to know about the Moodys?"

Landrum was ready with an answer. "I heard somebody mention them in the saloon last night, and I was trying to figure out if they're the same bunch I used to known down around Sweetwater."

Watts rubbed his jaw in thought. "I don't know if these Moodys have ever lived in West Texas or not. There are four boys in the family. Arlie is the oldest, and I can't even recall the names of the others. Their mother is still alive, too, and I believe she lives with them."

Landrum shook his head. "Nope, that's not the same family I used to know. They had all gals. Pretty ones, too." He grinned at Watts.

Watts laughed shortly. "No one would call any of these Moodys pretty," he said. "They're a rough lot. According to the rumors, they keep squaws and brew whiskey. I've heard that they have a cabin somewhere up in the Brakes, but unless they know you, it's worth your life to ride near there."

"Quick on the trigger, eh?" Landrum mused. Talking to Watts like this had been a lucky break, and he felt more certain that ever now that he was on the right trail.

"I wouldn't go up there," Watts said fervently. "Not even the Rangers go into the Brakes much. No need to. There's nothing there except a few hermits like the Moodys."

Watts was just echoing what Landrum had learned

in the saloon the night before. Landrum nodded and said, "Sounds like a bad bunch, all right."

"Say, speaking of O'Leary's place," Watts said, "I heard about Ab Huddleston. That was a horrible thing to witness, I imagine."

"It was," Landrum agreed, his demeanor abruptly turning grim. "From what I heard, folks are worried that this means the beginning of another outbreak of Indian trouble."

"That's what I'm afraid of." Watts shook his head. "It's a shame people can't live without fear of being murdered by savages. That's what keeps this country from developing to its full potential."

"I was told they come down off the reservations up in Indian Territory, carry out their raids, and run back home."

"That's right. And the army doesn't seem to give a damn!"

That wasn't strictly true, Landrum thought. If there had not been concern over the situation, Powell's Army never would have been sent in. But he couldn't correct the banker's angry assertion, not without revealing his true identity.

And he wasn't going to do that, not when he sensed that the case was drawing to a conclusion. Once he had proof that the Moodys were the ones smuggling whiskey into the Nations and had located their headquarters, he could pass the information on to Amos Powell. Powell could then work through channels and have troops sent in to break up the operation.

For a moment, Landrum wondered where Glidinghawk was and what he was doing. For all Landrum

139

knew, the Omaha was still at Fort Supply. He didn't like having the team split up like this. Somehow it made him nervous not to be able to keep an eye on what the others were doing—especially Fox.

To Watts, Landrum said, "Well, we can hope the Indians aren't going on a widespread rampage again. I don't intend to move on for a while."

"I just hope that the other citizens have your fortitude, Mr. Davis. If things get bad enough, Truscott could turn into a ghost town overnight."

Landrum shook his head. "It'll take more than a bunch of redskins to run me off."

He bid good morning to Watts and continued on down the street to O'Leary's place. The front door of the Shamrock was open and the swamper was sweeping out the saloon. Landrum stepped past him and went into the cool dimness of the big room.

O'Leary was behind the bar, a ledger spread open in front of him. He was laboriously adding up a long column of figures, occasionally licking the tip of the pencil he held in his knobby fingers. Glancing up at Landrum, he grunted, "Morning. We'll not be open for business for a short while yet, Mr. Davis. I can pour a small dram for ye, unofficial-like, if ye want."

Landrum shook his head. "No, thanks. Have you heard how the Huddleston boy is doing?"

O'Leary finished his mathematics and closed the ledger. "He's doing as well as can be expected, I suppose. He stayed with Hughie last night. The funeral for his poor father will be this afternoon. If the lad gets through that, I imagine he'll be all right."

Landrum nodded, looking suitably solemn. He

140

leaned on the bar and glanced at the open door of the saloon. Morning light spilled in through it, and the motes of dust stirred up by the swamper's sweeping danced crazily in the sunshine.

In a low voice, Landrum said, "Mr. O'Leary, I'm going to be honest with you. My funds are dwindling, and I'm on the lookout for a way to make some money. You know the Moodys, don't you?"

The elderly Irishman shot a sharp frown toward Landrum. "I heard ye talking to Garrick about the Moodys last night. I thought ye had more sense than to get mixed up with scoundrels like them, though."

Landrum shrugged. "When a man needs money, he can't always choose his associates."

"What makes ye think I know anything about the Moodys?" O'Leary asked, squinting across the bar.

"I hear they make whiskey," Landrum said bluntly. "You sell whiskey."

O'Leary bristled. "I have my stock brought in, and it's all good-quality liquor. I'm no peddler of inferior whiskey, Mr. Davis."

Quickly, Landrum tried to soothe the old man's ruffled feelings. "I know that," he said. "But there are bound to be times when you run a little short. And you can't tell me that all of these cowhands around here are experts on whiskey. Hell, we both know they'll drink damn near anything with a kick to it."

"Aye, that's the truth," O'Leary admitted. He looked around the barroom, empty except for the two of them. "I wouldn't admit this if anyone else was around, lad, but you're right. There are times I have to supplement my regular supply with that concoction brewed

141

up by the Moodys. I don't like it, but you're right about some of my customers. They don't know any difference, and they wouldn't care if they did."

"So you can tell me where to find the Moodys?" Landrum asked, trying to sound very interested but not *too* eager.

"Why? Why do ye want to see those scrufulous young assassins?"

"Let's just say I have some business I want to discuss with them."

O'Leary sighed. "All right, lad, be mysterious if ye like. 'Tis none of my affair, anyway. But I like you, and I don't want you to get yourself shot up by messing with the Moodys."

"I can take care of myself," Landrum declared, his features taut and angry. "If you don't want to tell me, I'll just ride out there and find them anyway. How hard can it be?"

"Hard enough to get ye ventilated, you young fool!" O'Leary snapped.

Landrum wondered how long it had been since someone had called him a young fool. No one had referred to him as young in quite a while. . . .

"If you're stubborn enough to go out into the Brakes, I'd best tell you what to look for," O'Leary said reluctantly. "Otherwise, ye'll never find the place, and even if ye did, the Moodys would start shooting before you could tell them why you're there."

"Thanks, Mr. O'Leary," Landrum said sincerely. "I appreciate it."

O'Leary scowled. "I'm only doing this because I feel sorry for that young lass with you. I don't want you getting killed and leaving her alone out here."

Quickly, the old man told Landrum how to find the Moodys. He detailed the route leading northwest from the town, and went on to say, "When ye come to the canyon that leads through the bluffs, ye'd best stop and fire three shots into the air. More than likely, one of the Moodys will be on guard there and will come to see what you want. You tell them that I sent you."

"Will that get you into trouble with them?"

O'Leary gave a short, barking laugh. "I'm too old to be worrying about such things, me boy. The Moodys don't frighten me."

Landrum nodded. "All right. Thanks again."

"Don't mention it. If ye want to pay me back, just try not to get yourself killed."

"I'll try," Landrum promised with a chuckle. He rang a coin on the shining bartop. "Now I could use a little hair of the dog, Mr. O'Leary."

The Irishman reached for a bottle. "I think I'll join ye. And this stuff, lad, was *not* purchased from the Moodys. I can promise ye that."

Landrum tossed off the drink and immediately felt much better. His headache vanished. He didn't know if that was because of the liquor or because he was excited about closing in on his quarry.

By the time he left O'Leary's, he was more than ready to ride.

He had to go by the house first, though, and let Celia know what he was doing. He also wanted to pass along to her the directions that O'Leary had given him. It was important that she know how to find the Moody place, in case anything happened to him. That way, at least the army could still come in and smash the smuggling scheme —

Even if he never came back from this ride.

CHAPTER FIFTEEN

"You're going to do what?" Celia asked. She was frowning in disapproval.

"I'm going to ride out into the Brakes and find the Moodys," Landrum told her. "I'm sure they're the ones behind the whiskey smuggling, and all I have to do now is find their headquarters."

"Oh. That's all," Celia snorted sarcastically.

Landrum checked the cinch of the saddle on the horse he had just rented at Truscott's only livery stable. The animal was a bay mare, not fast or flashy but dependable according to the stableman. Landrum patted the horse on the flank.

"This is crazy, Landrum," Celia said. She was standing in the small front yard of the Stanley house.

"Why?" he asked in genuine puzzlement. "You knew all along why we were here. We came to stop the whiskey runners. This is the best way to go about it."

"And you know what O'Leary told you. They're trigger-happy lunatics. You're going to get yourself killed."

Perhaps unwisely, Landrum had repeated the details of his conversations with Watts and O'Leary.

When she had heard what the banker and the saloon-keeper had to say, Celia had agreed with all of Landrum's conclusions — up to the point when he told her he was riding into the Brakes.

"We're in a risky business, Celia," Landrum pointed out. "Anyway, I remember somebody else taking some pretty foolish chances up in Denver while Glidinghawk and I weren't around."

Celia flushed, partly in anger and partly in embarrassment. "That was different," she said. "Like you said, you weren't there. I had an opportunity to crack the case and had to make the decision right away whether or not to take it. It worked out all right, didn't it?"

Landrum smiled humorlessly. "After a little gunfire, yeah, I suppose it did."

"You may run into more than a little gunfire out there, Landrum."

The Texan swung up into the saddle. "Maybe so. The important thing is that you remember those directions O'Leary gave me and I gave you. If I'm not back by tomorrow morning, you light out for the nearest town with a telegraph station and get in touch with Amos. Tell him to tell the cavalry to come a-runnin'."

Celia reached out and placed a hand on his thigh. It was a rather forward gesture, she knew, and if any of the ladies in the neighborhood were watching, they would be scandalized.

But what the hell, her reputation in this town was

a bad one to start with. To the citizens of Truscott, Landrum was some sort of rascal and Celia was his scarlet woman. Those were the images they had worked to project.

"If you're determined to do this, the least you can do is promise me you'll be careful," she said solemnly.

"Always," Landrum said with a grin.

"Huh! I know better, Landrum Davis."

He swung the horse around. "You just remember what I told you. Tomorrow morning, you hear?"

"I hear," Celia replied softly as he heeled the horse into motion. She watched him ride down the street and out of town, and she didn't go back in the house until he was completely out of sight.

Landrum was touched by Celia's concern, even though he didn't show it. Ever since he had met her, he had thought that if he were only a few years younger, he might have given in to the feelings he had for her.

He was a couple of decades older than her, however, and he had little to offer a young woman like Celia. Besides, they had formed a good working partnership. Romance would just cause unnecessary complications.

The terrain became more rugged as Landrum rode northwestward. Overall, it was still fairly flat, but the land began to be cut by gullies and marked by rocky red bluffs. Gradually, Landrum found himself riding through an area of almost complete desolation, an alien land where only fools would attempt to live.

Fools—or someone with something to hide.

Landrum's back was getting itchy, a feeling he recognized. He was being watched. Either that, or the stories he had heard about the Moodys back in Truscott had made him nervous.

He kept riding. At this point, there was nothing else he could do.

By the middle of the afternoon, he began to wonder if he had taken a wrong turn somewhere and gotten lost. Landrum thought he had followed O'Leary's directions correctly, noting what few landmarks there were out here, but by now he should have reached the canyon leading into the little valley where the Moodys had their cabin.

Just as that thought crossed his mind, he spotted the arroyo up ahead that quickly deepened into a cut that led deeper into the Brakes. That was what he was looking for, Landrum realized.

That was where the Moodys would have their guard, ready to challenge any strangers—and ready to shoot.

Landrum took a deep breath, still feeling that itchy sensation in the middle of his back, and put the horse into the cut. Its hoofbeats rang hollowly against the steep sides of the declivity.

Fifteen minutes went by while Landrum followed the narrow, winding canyon. He began to feel uncomfortably closed in by the walls, but he had come this far. Damned if he was going to turn back now.

The confines of the canyon became even tighter,

but he thought he could see it opening up somewhat ahead of him. Landrum kept the horse moving. . . .

And then the click of a hammer being drawn back, surprisingly loud in the hot afternoon silence, made him pull his mount to an abrupt halt.

"Sit easy, stranger," a voice said, "or I'll blow you right out of that saddle."

Gerald Glidinghawk was sitting in a little niche that nature had carved into the side of the canyon at some time in the dim past. There was a good-sized boulder perched on the narrow ledge to provide cover. It was a natural sentry post because it commanded a view of the canyon's entire width at a fairly narrow point.

One man with enough ammunition could almost hold off an army from up here.

Glidinghawk had been taking his turn at guard duty here for a couple of days now, and he had rapidly discovered that it was a boring job. However, it was better than staying around the cabin and trying to keep out of Ma Moody's sight. He forced himself to remain alert, because Arlie Moody had a habit of checking up on him. Now, as he rested his back against the rock, he heard Arlie puffing slightly as he climbed the trail to the sentry post.

Glidinghawk straightened a little, lifting the Winchester in his hands. It was possible that someone besides Arlie was trying to sneak up on him and doing a bad job of it. That was unlikely, though.

Arlie's battered black Stetson came into view. The

burly smuggler pulled himself up onto the ledge, his chest heaving as he tried to catch his breath. "Damn!" he exclaimed between gasps. "Man's nearly got to be a blamed mountain goat to get up here!"

Glidinghawk nodded. "Everything is quiet," he said.

"Any sign of Dirk yet?"

"I haven't seen him," Glidinghawk replied with a shake of his head. "Haven't seen anyone, in fact."

Dirk Moody had left the valley early that morning, heading for Truscott to buy some supplies. He would probably be returning soon.

"Hope he didn't have no trouble," Arlie said as he leaned against the side of the bluff and scanned the floor of the canyon. "Claude like to got in a fight a week or so ago while him and Dirk was there. I've told them boys to be careful in the saloon, but you know how youngsters are."

"Yes," Glidinghawk grunted wryly, thinking that Arlie made his brothers sound like mischievous boys rather than the brutal hardcases that they actually were.

" 'Course, Claude always did have a hankerin' for redheads. A real purty one came into town, and Claude just asked her to sit with him whilst he played some poker. Feller she was with took exception to the offer."

Glidinghawk kept his features under control, but he felt a quickening of his pulse and his interest. Arlie was just talking to hear the sound of his voice, but he might have unwittingly just given Glidinghawk some news about Landrum and Celia. He supposed some other pretty young redhead besides Celia could have arrived in Truscott a week earlier, but it wasn't very likely.

And Landrum Davis was the type to get his back up if Celia had been accosted by a lout like Dirk Moody.

Evidently the clash had not led to gunfire, which was good to hear if it had indeed been Landrum and Celia who were involved. Glidinghawk had wondered many times in the past couple of days how they were proceeding with their investigation. The knowledge that they were probably within a day's ride of him was frustrating.

Glidinghawk suddenly lifted his head. His keen ears had heard something, although he couldn't identify the sound over the noise of Arlie's yammering. He made a sharp slashing motion with his hand.

Arlie fell silent with a frown, clearly not caring for the way Glidinghawk had interrupted him. Then the displeasure on his face was replaced by a look of concentration.

"You hear it, too?" Glidinghawk asked in a voice that was little more than a whisper.

Arlie nodded. "Somebody comin'," he said. It was hard for him to moderate his gravelly tones, but he tried.

The sound of a horse came floating down the canyon. The animal was coming steadily toward them,

151

not hurrying.

Arlie grunted. "Probably just Dirk," he said, relaxing.

"Dirk would have called out by now to let whoever was on guard know he was coming," Glidinghawk pointed out. "That's the rule, isn't it?"

"Yeah, it is." Arlie's frown returned. "Reckon it must be somebody else. Either that, or somebody's got the drop on Dirk and is tryin' to get in with him as a hostage."

"Why would anyone want to do that?"

Arlie jerked a thumb toward the valley. "Ain't you got any idea what the whiskey stored back there is worth? Hell, there's a couple dozen full barrels there in the shack with the still. Some folks'd kill us all for a mess o' booze like that."

Glidinghawk twisted slightly, altering his position so that he could poke the muzzle of the Winchester past the boulder. Arlie crouched down beside him, sliding his Colt from its holster. Both men waited as the sound of approaching hoofbeats grew steadily louder. The rider would be coming into view any second. . . .

He rode around a bend in the canyon, a tall lean man in a broad-brimmed, flat-crowned hat. He wore brown whipcord pants and a tan shirt with the sleeves rolled up a turn. The legs of the pants were stuffed into high black boots. The man sat the saddle with the ease of a born rider.

Glidinghawk knew the craggy face almost as well

as he knew his own.

Landrum Davis.

Beside Glidinghawk, Arlie rumbled, "Who the hell is that?" and started to lift his gun.

Several thoughts flashed through the Omaha's mind. Arlie was likely to shoot first and ask questions later, after he had put a slug into Landrum. Also, Arlie would probably be watching to see what Glidinghawk's reaction would be to this intrusion. He had to move rapidly, both to save Landrum's life and to maintain his cover identity.

Snapping the Winchester to his shoulder, Glidinghawk called in a strong voice, "Sit easy, stranger, or I'll blow you right out of that saddle."

Landrum reined in abruptly. Even at this distance, Glidinghawk could see the surprise on the Texan's face and knew that Landrum had recognized his voice. But he also seemed to catch on quickly. As soon as the horse came to a stop, Landrum lifted his hands to show that he was peaceful.

Out of the corner of his eye, Glidinghawk could see Arlie watching him. He could not read the desperado's face, but at least Arlie had not opened fire on Landrum.

"Keep 'im covered," Arlie snapped.

Landrum raised his voice and said, "I'm not looking for trouble." His voice echoed in the narrow canyon. His eyes scanned the sides of the cut, trying to locate the person who had challenged him.

"Ask him what he's lookin' for," Arlie commanded.

Glidinghawk complied. "Who are you, and what do you want?" he called down, keeping the rifle trained on his partner.

"Name's Landrum Davis. I'm looking for some folks named Moody."

Arlie grunted in surprise. He stood up, leveling his Colt at Landrum, and asked, "Who sent you, mister?"

Coolly, Landrum replied, "Nobody sent me. I came on my own. A fella told me how to find the place."

"Who?"

Landrum shook his head. "I don't seem to recollect just who it was. But he told me that the Moodys might have some liquor for sale." His head tilted back, Landrum studied the burly man holding a gun on him and then went on, "You must be Arlie Moody."

Arlie frowned. "What if I am?"

"The man I talked to said you were the head man out here, said I should talk to you." Landrum moved his hands slightly. "Is it all right to put my arms down now, since that heathen savage behind the rock there has a rifle pointed at me?"

Glidinghawk suppressed the grin that tried to pull at his mouth. So Landrum had spotted him. Well, that was no surprise.

"All right, all right." Arlie waved for him to lower his arms. "Now what's this you're sayin' about whiskey?"

154

"If you're selling, I'm looking to buy."

"For yourself?"

"I'm opening a new saloon in Truscott. I need a steady supply of good cheap liquor. These cow nurses up here won't know the difference."

Arlie laughed, that harsh barking sound that Glidinghawk had come to know and despise. "You must be a pretty brave feller to come ridin' out here like this—or a damned stupid one."

Glidinghawk heard the sound of another horse coming. Neither Landrum nor Arlie seemed to notice it over their own conversation, but the Omaha wasn't surprised when Dirk Moody appeared behind Landrum. His pistol was in his hand, and as he pointed it at Landrum, he yelled up, "Don't worry, Arlie! I got the drop on him!"

"Hell, I ain't worried," Arlie replied to his brother. "We got the bastard covered ourselves."

Glidinghawk saw Landrum glance over his shoulder at Dirk. Landrum had to be wondering just what he had ridden into. He probably hadn't known that Dirk was also on his way to the valley from Truscott and would ride into the canyon behind him. Landrum must have uncovered the same information from his end of the investigation—that the Moodys were responsible for distilling and smuggling the illegal whiskey.

"Look, I came out here to talk business," Landrum said now, somewhat testily. "I don't much like doing it from the back of a horse with a bunch of guns pointed at me. If you don't want to sell any liquor to me, I'll find my supply elsewhere."

He started to turn his horse's head, but Dirk spurred closer and jabbed the barrel of his Colt into Landrum's back. "Hold it, mister!" he said sharply. "Arlie ain't said you could leave, and nobody get out of here without Arlie's say-so."

Glidinghawk glanced up at Arlie, saw that he was pondering the situation. With a nod to himself, Arlie finally said, "Back off there, Dirk. Let the man ride on. We got business to talk over."

"That's more like it," Landrum said, as Dirk frowned and looked reluctant to follow Arlie's orders.

"Glidinghawk, you come with me," Arlie said. Turning back to the canyon, he called, "Dirk, you leave your hoss and that pack mule and come up here. I want you to relieve Glidinghawk."

"Aw hell, Arlie, I just rode all the way back from town!" Dirk protested. "And half the way I was folland tryin' to see what he was up to. There's somethin' familiar about him." The burly young man sleeved sweat off his forehead. "I'm tired. I need a drink."

"You need to do what I tell you, dammit!" Arlie howled. He jerked the barrel of his Colt toward Dirk and squeezed off a round. The slug whipped past the younger man and then whined off down the canyon, ricocheting from one of the stony walls.

Dirk scrambled to follow orders. Arlie told Glidinghawk to take charge of Dirk's horse and the pack mule.

When they reached the floor of the canyon, Arlie kept his gun in his hand as he approached Landrum. Landrum looked past him for the barest of moments and let his gaze meet that of Glidinghawk. The instant was fleeting, but it was enough to let both men know that they would play along with whatever the other one wanted.

Arlie said, "I'll trouble you for that hogleg, mister. Just bein' careful, you understand."

Reaching across his body and using his left hand, Landrum slipped his gun out and handed it over. "A man can't be too careful," he agreed.

That was the truth, Glidinghawk thought.

He and Landrum were both going to have to be damned careful, if they were going to live through this afternoon.

CHAPTER SIXTEEN

Glidinghawk took the reins of Dirk's horse and the pack mule and started leading them down the canyon behind Landrum and Arlie. Landrum had dismounted and was leading his own horse.

Dirk gave Glidinghawk an angry look as the Omaha passed him. It was clear that Dirk resented the way Arlie had come to trust and rely on Glidinghawk almost overnight. Claude was the same way, Glidinghawk knew. He had no friends here, with the possible exception of Sun Woman.

And she had been avoiding him about as diligently as he had been steering clear of Ma Moody.

Was it because she didn't trust herself to be around him? Was she afraid she would give in to her feelings if she found herself too close to him?

Arlie led the way out of the canyon and into the valley. Glidinghawk couldn't see Landrum's face, but he knew the Texan would be taking in all the details of the scene—the cabins, the sheer walls of the bluffs, the trail on the far side of the valley.

"Looks like quite a setup you've got here," Landrum said to Arlie.

"We've worked hard enough for it," Arlie grunted.

"What'd you say your name was again?"

"Landrum Davis."

"Texan, ain't you?"

"Yep. I've traveled around a lot, but I was born down close to San Antone."

Arlie spat. "Lots of greasers down there, ain't there?"

"Too many," Landrum replied with a harsh laugh. He glanced over his shoulder, his eyes meeting Glidinghawk's for an instant. Glidinghawk nodded slightly, trying to convey his opinion that Landrum was approaching Arlie with the right attitude.

If there was some way they could both get out of here now, their job would be over. The army could handle the mopping up.

But that was unlikely. Arlie might trust him, but there would be limits to that trust. He would probably want Glidinghawk to stay where he could keep an eye on him.

Which meant he would have to slip out of the canyon secretly. Glidinghawk was confident he could do that.

But what would happen to Sun Woman and the other squaws when the cavalry came boiling in here to wipe out the Moodys' liquor operation?

Glidinghawk had an uneasy feeling in the pit of his stomach when he thought about that.

The three men walked up to the main cabin. Arlie told Landrum to tie his horse at the hitch rail, while Glidinghawk led Dirk's animals to the corral. He wished he could go on in the cabin with Arlie and Landrum, but he knew he would be expected to unload the supplies from the mule.

When he had Dirk's horse unsaddled, he untied the box of supplies from the mule and hoisted it onto his shoulder. He went to the back door of the cabin and pushed it open with his foot.

Sun Woman was in the kitchen. She looked up as Glidinghawk came in, and as usual, she immediately turned her gaze away.

"Here are the things Dirk brought from town," he said.

"Thank you," Sun Woman murmured, still not looking at him.

Glidinghawk put the box down on the rude table in the center of the room, then turned toward the door into the cabin's main room. "Where's Ma?" he asked in a low voice.

"Ma Moody sit with Benton," Sun Woman told him.

"Arlie and the stranger are in there alone?"

Sun Woman nodded. "Claude is out at still with squaws." She glanced up. "You know stranger?"

Glidinghawk shook his head. "Never saw him until he rode up the canyon just now," he lied. Even though he was sympathetic to Sun Woman's plight, he wasn't ready to trust her with his secret.

He pushed on through the door into the main room. Arlie and Landrum were sitting across from each other, each of them holding a drink of the

Moody whiskey.

"I brought in the supplies," Glidinghawk said as Arlie looked up at him. "Do you want me to go back to the canyon now and take Dirk's place?"

"Leave him out there," Arlie replied. "Pull up a chair, Glidinghawk. Unless Mr. Davis here minds talkin' business with you around."

Landrum shook his head. He had taken off his hat and placed it on the floor beside his chair. He looked relaxed and at ease. "I don't mind," he said.

"Glidinghawk here is right smart . . . for an Injun," Arlie said. "He ain't been workin' with us for long, but he's come in handy a few times."

"Thanks," Glidinghawk said dryly as he pulled a chair over to sit down.

"He's one of them educated Injuns," Arlie said with a grin.

Landrum raised his glass and nodded to Glidinghawk. "To your health, sir."

"I'd return the toast, but I'm not allowed to sample the white man's firewater."

"Now, I explained that to you, Glidinghawk," Arlie said. "You redskins just can't handle the stuff. I don't mind sellin' it to them bucks up on the reservations, but I ain't goin' to have no drunken Injun workin' for me."

"It's all right, Arlie," Glidinghawk told him. "You and Mr. Davis just go on with your business."

Arlie turned back to Landrum. "Just how many barrels do you think you'll be needin' when you get

161

this here saloon of yours open?" he asked.

For the next few minutes, Landrum and Arlie discussed their potential arrangement. Knowing Landrum as well as he did, Glidinghawk had a feeling that the Texan was making up the details of this saloon deal as he went along. But everything Landrum said made sense, and it was unlikely that Arlie would see through the ruse.

Greed had warred with caution inside Arlie, and the desire for a new steady customer had won. When Landrum said, "I think we've got a deal," and stuck out his hand, Arlie shook it happily, a broad grin on his ugly face.

Now Landrum could get out of this place and head back to Truscott with the information he needed to wrap up this mission. All that would be left for Glidinghawk to do would be to get out of the valley himself.

The Omaha heard the back door of the cabin open and heavy footsteps cross the kitchen. Claude Moody pushed into the room, his usual frown on his face, and Glidinghawk suddenly remembered what Arlie had been talking about out there in the canyon.

Claude had had trouble in Truscott with someone that Glidinghawk thought was likely Landrum Davis.

And now Landrum was sitting right here in the cabin, a big grin on his face.

Claude's surly gaze fell on the newcomer, and recognition flashed in his eyes. "You!" he spat.

His hand flashed toward the gun on his hip.

Glidinghawk launched himself out of his chair as Arlie yelled, "No, Claude!" Landrum ducked to the side, his hand instinctively slapping at his empty holster.

Claude's pistol was just clearing leather when Glidinghawk rammed into him. The Omaha's shoulder drove into his belly, knocking him backward. The hand holding the Colt flailed wildly as Claude fell, and the heavy weapon blasted.

Glidinghawk landed on top of Claude. His fingers grappled for the wrist of the other man's gun hand. Glidinghawk got a good hold and twisted, and the gun dropped to the rough planks of the floor.

Arlie lunged at Landrum and grasped his arm. "Hold it!" Arlie barked. "Glidinghawk's got him!"

Claude was still struggling. He was bigger than Glidinghawk, and the Omaha realized he was no match for the other man in a brawl. He had to strike quickly and end this battle in a hurry.

Glidinghawk released his hold on Claude's wrist and brought his elbow across sharply, the point of it slamming into Claude's jaw. At the same time, Glidinghawk drove his knee up into Claude's groin.

A shriek of pain erupted from the man's mouth. Glidinghawk raised himself enough to get some striking room and lashed out with his right fist. The blow caught Claude on the chin, snapping his head back to bounce against the floor. Claude sighed heavily, and his body abruptly sagged.

Glidinghawk rolled away, springing to his feet in

case Claude wasn't knocked unconscious. He saw right away that that was an unnecessary precaution.

Claude Moody was out cold.

Glidinghawk lifted a shaking hand and wiped it across his mouth. If Claude had ever gotten those bearlike arms around him, he would have squeezed until breath — and life — were gone.

Glidinghawk glanced up and saw Arlie and Landrum watching him. Both men were tense, ready for violence.

When more came, it was from an unexpected source. The door to one of the bedrooms slammed open, and Ma Moody came rushing out, hair in wild disarray from the haste with which she was moving.

As her eyes fell on Claude, stretched out on the floor, she screeched, "Claude! The Injun done kilt him!"

Glidinghawk knew what was about to happen and darted for the door. He didn't make it before the old woman landed on his back, clawing and scratching and biting. He let out a yelp and tried to twist around to get his hands on her. He didn't want to hurt her, but she'd rip his eyes out if she got the chance.

"Ma!" Arlie yelled. "Claude's all right, Ma! He ain't dead!"

Ma Moody paid no attention to her oldest son. Glidinghawk was about to lose his temper and hit the insane old woman when Sun Woman suddenly appeared beside him. She wrapped her arms around

164

Ma and gently but firmly pulled her away. The old woman's weight seemed not to bother Sun Woman as she carried Ma toward the kitchen.

Arlie grabbed Glidinghawk's arm and rapped, "Come on! Let's get out of here."

He hustled the Omaha out onto the porch, Landrum following closely behind them and shutting the door. Glidinghawk leaned on the porch railing and tried to catch his breath while Arlie demanded, "What the hell was that all about?" He swung to face Landrum. "Why'd Claude throw down on you, mister?"

Landrum's muscles were still tensed. The potential for more trouble was still in the air. "I guess he recognized me from Truscott. I had a little run-in with him the day I arrived in town, about a week ago. I didn't know until just now that he was your brother, though."

Arlie nodded. "I reckon I heard about that ruckus. Claude always was one to go on the prod when a stranger come around."

"It didn't amount to anything," Landrum told him. "There was no shooting, not even a punch thrown. Come to think of it, your other brother was there, too. I thought I had seen him somewhere before." He nodded toward the line of bluffs on the south side of the valley.

From the canyon, Dirk came running, his rifle lifted, ready for trouble. As he pounded up, he gasped, "I heard a shot! What's wrong?"

Arlie bounded down from the porch, snagged Dirk's coat collar and shook his younger brother like a terrier shakes a rat. Leveling a finger at Landrum, Arlie roared, "Why the hell didn't you tell me this was the feller Claude had trouble with in town?"

"Aw hell, let go, Arlie!" Dirk protested. "I told you I thought he looked familiar. I just didn't recollect where I'd seen him before."

"Well, now you know," Arlie said disgustedly. "Claude come into the room, saw him, and went for his gun."

Dirk's eyes widened in anger and fear. "Where's Claude?" he demanded, jerking loose from Arlie's grip and swiveling his rifle toward Landrum. "If he's killed Claude, I'll blow a hole right through the bastard!"

Arlie grabbed the rifle barrel and pushed it aside. "Stop that, you damned fool! Claude's fine. Glidinghawk had the sense to jump him and knock him out when he tried to gun Mr. Davis here." Arlie frowned abruptly and turned toward the Omaha. "How'd you know to do that, Glidinghawk?"

Glidinghawk took a deep breath. His pulse was slowing down to normal now, and the blood wasn't pounding quite so loudly in his head. He said, "I knew you were planning to do business with Mr. Davis. I didn't figure you wanted Claude to shoot him before you completed the deal."

"Smart thinkin'," Arlie said, ignoring the sullen look Dirk gave him as he listened to the praise for the Indian. "Get back out there to the canyon, Dirk."

When Dirk was gone, reluctantly, Landrum said, "I reckon I'd better drift. It's going to get dark before I get back to Truscott unless I start soon."

"Sure, you go right ahead. When do you need that whiskey?"

"Better hold off a little while," Landrum said. "I've got my financing coming in to the Truscott bank soon. I'll be in touch with you again when the funds have arrived."

"That's fine," Arlie told him. "The boys know you now, you won't have no trouble gettin' in to see us."

"Not even if Claude is on guard duty?" Landrum asked shrewdly. "I wouldn't want him to accidentally put a half-dozen Winchester slugs into me."

"He won't," Arlie said, his voice hard as he handed Landrum back his gun. "I'll set Claude straight. Holdin' a grudge is one thing, business is another."

Landrum swung onto his horse and touched the brim of his hat. "Be seein' you," he said.

Glidinghawk had been listening to the conversation with great interest. Now he said to Arlie, "Wouldn't it be a good idea if I rode along with Mr. Davis to the other end of the canyon? You haven't had a chance to give Dirk any specific orders yet about letting Mr. Davis come and go."

"Not a bad idea," Arlie agreed after thinking it over for a moment. "Saddle up a hoss and go with him. If Dirk gives you any trouble, you tell him to come see me about it later."

Glidinghawk nodded and hurriedly threw his saddle on a horse. Landrum was waiting patiently when Glidinghawk rejoined him in front of the cabin.

Arlie lifted a hand to wave in farewell. "Lookin' forward to doin' business with you, Mr. Davis," he called as the two men rode off.

Glidinghawk kept his eyes to the front and didn't look at Landrum. But when they were out of earshot of the cabin and not yet close enough to the canyon for Dirk to hear them, Glidinghawk asked the question that had to be uppermost in their minds.

"What the hell do we do now?"

CHAPTER SEVENTEEN

Landrum lifted a hand to rub his jaw and answered without turning his head. "Well, I reckon when we get to the other end of that canyon, we can both light out."

"That won't work," Glidinghawk said flatly.

Landrum pondered the point for a moment, then said, "No, it won't. They'd know something was wrong if you took off like that, and I don't like the idea of having to hightail it back to Truscott across that wasteland with a family of bushwhackers after us."

"And even if we did get away, they'd be spooked then," Glidinghawk added. "They'd be liable to move deeper into the Brakes, and then the army would never be able to root them out."

Landrum sighed heavily. "I don't like it, but I reckon you've got to stay out here for the time being."

"That was my conclusion as well." Glidinghawk fell silent for a moment, then went on, "I like your story about wanting to open a saloon."

"Thought of it while I was riding out here today," Landrum replied. "It seemed like the best reason to be looking for somebody who makes whiskey. I suppose the Moodys are the ones smuggling the stuff into the Nations."

"They sure as hell are. They're in it with a supply sergeant named Foster up at Fort Supply. He's the one who recruited me to join the scheme."

"Is Fox around, too?"

"Still up at the fort, as far as I know," Glidinghawk replied. "He was keeping up his Indian agent masquerade when I broke out of the stockade. That's been several days, though, so I don't know what might have happened in the meantime."

A smile tugged at Landrum's wide mouth. "Broke out of the stockade?" he echoed.

Glidinghawk sighed. "It's a long story. It got the results we wanted. Anyway, I recall a little jailbreak in Dodge City that you were involved in."

"Don't remind me," Landrum said. Both of them remembered the devastation that had occurred when Preston Fox used a commandeered locomotive to bust Landrum out of the hoosegow and save him from a hanging.

They had reached the canyon, and they fell silent as they entered it. Voices could carry in the narrow confines, and they didn't want Dirk overhearing any of their discussion.

When they approached the sentry post, Dirk leveled his rifle at them and yelled, "Hold it! Where do you two think you're goin'?"

"Take it easy, Dirk," Glidinghawk called back. "Mr. Davis here is going back to Truscott. I'm just riding with him a little way so that there won't be any trouble."

"How do I know that's what Arlie wants?" Dirk demanded, continuing to menace them with the rifle.

"He said to tell you that if you've got any problem with it, to talk to him later." Glidinghawk shrugged. "You can do what you want, I suppose."

Dirk frowned. Hesitantly, he said, "I reckon you wouldn't be out here if'n it weren't all right with Arlie. But I'm warnin' you, redskin—just 'cause Arlie trusts you, that don't mean I'm goin' to."

"I don't expect you to," Glidinghawk said bluntly. "Just let us pass, all right?"

Dirk jerked the barrel of the Winchester to indicate that they should proceed. "Go ahead," he said, his tone surly and resentful.

"I'll be back in a few minutes," Glidinghawk told him as he and Landrum rode along the canyon floor beneath the sentry post. "Just thought I'd tell you, in case your trigger finger gets a little nervous." Meaningfully, he put his hand on the butt of his Colt.

Dirk snorted and settled back down behind the boulder without saying anything else.

Glidinghawk and Landrum rode in silence to the end of the canyon. The sun was starting its downward slide toward the western horizon as they emerged from the cut. Glidinghawk reined in and said, "Be careful. I don't think anyone will follow you, but keep an eye on your backtrail just in case."

"Always do," Landrum drawled. "I pure-dee hate to

leave you out here in the middle of this mess of snakes, Gerald."

"I'll be fine," Glidinghawk assured him. "Give my best to Celia."

"I'll do that. She'll be glad to know that you're all right." Landrum cuffed his hat back slightly and leaned on the pommel of his saddle as he went on, "I'll try to get word to Amos, and then I'll be back to let you know when the troops will be getting here. You'll want to be gone when the fireworks start."

Glidinghawk nodded. "But not before. We don't want the Moodys suspecting anything."

Landrum grinned. "Think you can stay out of the old woman's way for that long?"

"She's more dangerous than all the others," Glidinghawk said with a bitter laugh. "But I'll be fine. So long, Landrum."

"Adios," the Texan said. He wheeled his horse and spurred away, heading back toward Truscott.

Glidinghawk turned his mount, too, and started back down the canyon, back into — as Landrum had so aptly described it — that mess of snakes.

Arlie was waiting on the porch when Glidinghawk returned to the cabin. "Any trouble?" he asked as the Omaha dismounted.

"No. Dirk was a little proddy when we rode by him, but he didn't try to shoot anybody."

"Good," Arlie grunted. "Claude's comin' around, so

172

I reckon you'd better make yourself scarce for a while. I'll explain to him why you jumped him, but he still ain't goin' to be happy."

Glidinghawk nodded. He felt weariness tugging at his shoulders, but he knew what the best solution might be. "I'll go back out to the canyon and take over for Dirk," he said.

"Hell, you just got back from there. Besides, you've already taken your turn today."

"It doesn't matter," Glidinghawk said with a shrug. "I don't want any more trouble with Claude. Your brothers already don't like me, and your mother wants to kill me."

Arlie threw back his head and gave a braying laugh. "Reckon you ain't a member of the family yet, Glidinghawk. But what I say around here goes, and I think you've done a good job so far." The whiskey smuggler's face abruptly became more serious. "Just don't get no fancy ideas 'bout takin' over. I'm still the boss o' this deal."

Glidinghawk shook his head. "I don't want to take over anything, Arlie. When Benton's on his feet again, I just might drift on out of here."

"We'll see," Arlie said noncommittally.

"Let me get a drink, and then I'll head back to the canyon."

Glidinghawk didn't go into the cabin. He skirted it on his way to the well. After he had hauled up a bucket of water, he used the dipper that hung on the windlass frame to scoop up some to drink. It had a coppery taste that was rather unpleasant, but he was getting used to it. As he hung up the dipper when he was through, he glanced toward the cabin.

The back door was open, and Sun Woman was standing there gazing at him. When his eyes met hers, she turned away quickly and disappeared. Glidinghawk grimaced. The sight of her was a painful reminder that he had not figured out what to do about her and the other Indian women.

To be painfully honest, he thought, it was primarily Sun Woman he was worried about. He didn't want any harm coming to the other squaws, but ever since he had arrived here, he had felt something special for Sun Woman—an attraction that went beyond the fact of her beauty.

He had long since decided that the capacity for real love did not exist within him. Now he was not sure. Perhaps that was what he was feeling; perhaps it was only a mixture of pity and admiration and desire.

Glidinghawk wasn't sure about anything anymore. All he knew for certain was that this was an unresolved problem, something he would have to deal with before this mission came to a conclusion.

He went back to his horse, mounted up, and rode toward the canyon. Along the way, he tried to figure out how much time he had to come up with a solution.

Landrum would have to get to a telegraph station and send a coded wire to Amos Powell with the information about the Moodys. Then Amos could pass along the intelligence through the proper channels. But there was no way of knowing how long it would take troops to arrive in the vicinity. That would depend on where they were coming from and what other problems might be occupying their attention.

His brain still whirling, Glidinghawk brought the horse to a stop where the trail up to the lookout post began. Dirk glared down at him and asked, "What the hell're you doin' back out here, Injun?"

"Arlie said for you to come in. I'm taking your place."

"You've already stood your watch."

Glidinghawk waited at the bottom of the steep, narrow path. He wasn't going to start up it with Dirk waiting at the top. It would be too easy for the other man to topple him off the ledge and then claim it was an accident.

"It doesn't matter," Glidinghawk said. "I don't mind taking another turn."

"All right," Dirk said, and shrugged. He scrambled down the path and held out the Winchester to Glidinghawk. Taking the reins of Glidinghawk's horse, he started back toward the valley with no word of farewell or thanks.

That was no surprise. Any of the Moodys — with the lucky exception of Arlie — would have gladly put a bullet or a knife in him, Glidinghawk knew.

And Arlie would strike just as quickly as any of the others if he thought he was being double-crossed, the

Omaha thought.

As he climbed to the sentry post and settled down to wait behind the boulder, he wondered if he should take advantage of this opportunity to slip away. He could be long gone before anyone came out here to check on him.

But he would be on foot, and besides, as he had told Landrum, running out now would make Arlie suspicious. He couldn't chance setting out into the Brakes without a horse.

The sun was almost down now, and the canyon was already cloaked with deep shadows. Glidinghawk rested his back against the rock and closed his eyes. He knew he wouldn't go to sleep, but he could draw some rest from this position without any loss in alertness. His keen ears were still attuned for the slightest sound that might be out of place.

He heard the horse coming long before he saw it. The sound of slow, steady hoofbeats came from the valley, so it was unlikely that it represented a threat. Glidinghawk straightened, opened his eyes, and peered through the gloom that had dropped down with the coming of night. His sharp gaze picked out the horse moving along the floor of the canyon toward his position.

The lone rider brought the animal to a stop at the foot of the ledge and swung lithely out of the saddle. Glidinghawk heard the rustle of a buckskin dress, saw moonlight shining on midnight-dark hair.

Sun Woman climbed the path, using one hand

against the rocky wall to balance herself while she carried something in the other hand. When she reached the top, she extended the small basket she held to Glidinghawk.

"Food," she said simply.

Glidinghawk leaned the rifle in a fissure in the rock so that it couldn't fall over, then took the basket from her. The smell of fried chicken and hot biscuits came from it. He pushed back the cloth that covered the food and smiled.

"Thank you," he said. "This is wonderful. Did Arlie send you out here with this?"

Sun Woman shook her head. "Arlie not know. Sun Woman decide you probably hungry, bring food for you." She started to turn away, almost before the words were out of her mouth.

"Wait," Glidinghawk said. "Have you eaten yet? It looks like there's enough here for two."

Without looking at him, she said, "Sun Woman must go back."

Glidinghawk set the basket down beside him and came to his feet, reaching out to stop her. His hand grasped her arm, and he felt the warmth of her flesh under the buckskin.

He turned her around and put his other hand under her chin, lifting it so that he could see her face. She stared impassively at him. He said nothing, content for the moment to study her lovely features in the moonlight.

Finally, Sun Woman said, "You should not do

this."

"I have to," Glidinghawk breathed.

His mouth came down on hers.

For long seconds, she stood stiff and unresponsive in his arms, her lips closed and cold under his. But then, gradually, she began to lean against him. Her arms came up from where they had hung limply at her sides and stole around his waist. A low moan drifted from her throat.

Her lips opened, and suddenly her kiss was a burning, blazing thing, as if, true to her name, a sun had suddenly burst into life within her.

Glidinghawk stroked her hair, letting his hands stray down her back to the gentle curve of her hips. He felt himself responding, heat growing inside him to match what was suddenly coming from her.

The passion they felt was too great for either of them to deny any longer. Mixed in with the tumult of emotions coursing through them was more than a little desperation. Both of them were trapped by who and what they were.

For the moment, though, they would find an escape in each other.

The rocky ledge should have been uncomfortable. But as they sank down on it, hands groping at their clothes and pushing all the barriers aside, neither of them noticed any discomfort.

All they felt was each other, and the inferno that threatened to consume them.

An unknowable time later, Glidinghawk sat against the cliff face with Sun Woman cradled in his arms, her head resting on his chest. There was a sense of contentment within him, yet he knew that it couldn't last.

"I suppose you'd better get back to the cabin," he said softly. "Arlie's probably missed you by now."

Sun Woman nodded but said nothing.

A bittersweet smile crossed Glidinghawk's face. "The food's probably cold by now, too, but cold chicken's not bad. Sure you don't want some of it?"

"Sun Woman bring for you," she whispered.

"You brought me much more than that." Glidinghawk frowned as the problems of the moment came crowding back into his mind. "Sun Woman, I know you're not happy here. Would you be willing to leave?"

She lifted her head so that she could look up at him. "With you?" she asked simply.

Glidinghawk nodded.

"Sun Woman go," she said.

Glidinghawk took a deep breath. He didn't know how things would work out, but at least he had an objective now. He would get the hell out of this valley once Landrum warned him that the cavalry was on the way, and he would take Sun Woman with him.

"We can't go now," he told her. "But soon. And it's very important that no one else know about this, especially not Arlie."

She shook her head. "Sun Woman not talk to Arlie unless she has to. Arlie not good man. Not like Glidinghawk is good man."

He laughed softly. "I'm glad you feel that way." Patting her on the rump, he went on, "You'd better go now."

Sun Woman stood up, unfolding herself reluctantly from Glidinghawk's embrace. She stretched, and she looked so appealing that Glidinghawk had to take her into his arms again for another quick kiss.

His lips had just met hers when a fusillade of gunfire erupted from the valley, splitting the night with its explosions.

CHAPTER EIGHTEEN

Instinctively, Glidinghawk whirled around, thrusting Sun Woman behind him so as to shield her with his own body. He drew the Colt on his hip, crouching slightly as his reflexes took over.

The shots were not coming from anywhere close by, though. As Glidinghawk listened, he could tell that the gunfire was originating from the vicinity of the cabin. And from the volume of it, a small war was going on.

"What the hell . . . ?" he muttered.

Sun Woman clutched at the sleeve of his buckskin shirt. "We go," she said urgently. "This bad."

He knew she was probably right, but at the same time, he felt as if he had to know what was happening back in the valley. He had been assigned to locate the source of the whiskey trade and help destroy it, and he couldn't just ride away now.

"I've got to go back," he said in a low-pitched voice.

"You not help Moodys," Sun Woman pleaded. "We go now."

Glidinghawk shook his head. "I can't." He bent over and scooped up the basket of food she had brought to him. As he handed it back to her, he said softly, "I'm sorry."

Sun Woman took the basket in silence.

Glidinghawk sighed and picked up the rifle. He started down the trail to the canyon floor, glancing behind him occasionally to make sure that Sun Woman was following him.

The shooting stopped when they were about halfway down the trail. Glidinghawk paused and listened, and in the silence that followed, he thought he heard something. He frowned, shook his head, and wondered if he had lost his senses.

The sound of laughter came from the valley.

"Come on," he hissed to Sun Woman.

When they reached the floor of the canyon, Glidinghawk caught the reins of the horse Sun Woman had ridden out there. He could still hear a bray of laughter from time to time, coming from the area of the cabin.

"You stay here," Glidinghawk said to Sun Woman as he mounted the horse. "If there's trouble, you can hide and slip away later. I don't think anybody will find you in these Brakes."

"Sun Woman go with Glidinghawk," she replied stubbornly. Before he could stop her, she grasped the saddle horn and swung up behind him.

"Dammit, woman—" he began.

"You want to see what happen in valley," she snapped. "We ride."

Muttering under his breath, Glidinghawk heeled the horse into motion. He would let her have her way

182

for the moment, but when they got close enough to the cabin to see what was going on, she would have to let him proceed alone. He wasn't going to risk her life if he could help it.

They rode out of the canyon at a gallop, the horse carrying its double load effortlessly. Glidinghawk halfway expected to see the cabin ablaze, but no fires lit the night. Everything looked fairly normal, in fact, except for the fact that the cabin door was open, spilling more light than usual from the lanterns inside. Dark figures crossed frequently in front of the light.

"Something's going on, all right," Glidinghawk murmured to himself, his soft words carried away in the rush of wind around their heads. As they got close to the cabin, he could distinguish a large group of horses near it.

Slowing their own mount to a halt, Glidinghawk told Sun Woman, "All right, this is as far as you go. Slide off. I'll come back to get you if everything is all right."

"No," Sun Woman replied sharply. For such a submissive squaw a few hours earlier, she had become increasingly stubborn, Glidinghawk thought.

The budding argument was abruptly rendered pointless. Several dark forms suddenly appeared from the scrubby brush that covered the valley floor. Glidinghawk stiffened in the saddle as the moonlight illuminated the half-naked bodies and the rifles in their hands—rifles that were pointed at the two riders.

Glidinghawk heard Sun Woman gasp in surprise, but thankfully she had the presence of mind to remain as motionless as he did. One of the Indian braves called out to them in a guttural tongue. Kiowa, Glidinghawk thought. In English, Glidinghawk said to Sun Woman, "Do you know what he said?"

"He want to know who we are, what we do here."

That was what Glidinghawk had thought from what little of the dialect he had understood. Holding the reins in one hand, he raised the other, palm out, in the sign of peace. In his native Omaha, he said, "We are friends." Maybe one of the grim-faced warriors would understand the words, or at least the intent.

The cabin was about a hundred and fifty yards away. Glidinghawk saw a bulky, familiar figure step out onto the porch. Arlie Moody seemed to be looking out toward them, and a moment later, Glidinghawk heard him call, "Hey, what's goin' on out there?"

Arlie didn't sound upset or worried. Glidinghawk hesitated, unsure what to do next. The events of the last few minutes had left him completely confused. Finally, he raised his voice and shouted, "It's Glidinghawk, Arlie!"

A figure in a feathered headdress appeared beside Arlie. Arlie turned to him and spoke quickly, and a moment later, harsh commands in Kiowa came floating out to the sentries who had gotten the drop on Glidinghawk and Sun Woman. One of the braves jerked the barrel of his rifle toward the cabin in an unmistakable gesture of command. It was an order Glidinghawk was glad to obey.

He kept the horse to a slow walk as the group proceeded toward the cabin. The guards had the animal almost totally surrounded, and Glidinghawk knew he wouldn't have been able to make it ten feet if he tried to break away. They would blast him — and Sun Woman — out of the saddle if he tried anything, even in these shadows.

As Glidinghawk rode up in front of the porch, he saw Arlie talking animatedly with the Kiowa chief. Both men had jugs of whiskey in their hands and were taking frequent slugs from them. Arlie's face was ruddy in the lantern light.

Arlie looked up at Glidinghawk with a grin. "You must've wondered what the hell was goin' on when the shootin' started. If I'd've knowed that Brass Hand here was comin', I'd've warned you, Glidinghawk."

So the Kiowa chief was Brass Hand, Glidinghawk thought. He had heard of the man. Brass Hand was thought to be a renegade, but it had never been proven that he led his men on bloody raids south of the Red River.

Dryly, Glidinghawk said, "I thought the cabin was being attacked."

"Nope, just Brass Hand and his boys sayin' hello. They come ridin' in from the north every now and then for a little fandango." Arlie lifted his jug. "They know how to celebrate. Reckon we figgered it was all

185

over when they started circlin' 'round the cabin and lettin' off all them shots."

Suddenly, the smile on Arlie's face turned into a frown as he gazed past Glidinghawk's shoulder.

"Who's that with you?" he demanded.

Before Glidinghawk could reply, Sun Woman slid down from the saddle and faced Arlie with a haughty look on her face. "I take food to sentry post," she said. "Man get hungry out there."

"Did I tell you to do that?" Arlie demanded. "I wondered where the hell you'd got off to."

"No, you not tell Sun Woman to go," she answered.

"Then git inside!" Arlie ordered harshly. "We got company to feed!"

Sun Woman hesitated, then lowered her head and obeyed Arlie's command. For a moment, Glidinghawk had thought she was going to defy him, but the training of long years had finally won out. Sun Woman was just too accustomed to doing whatever her man told her to do.

Arlie looked speculatively up at Glidinghawk. "I been takin' your side ever since you joined up with us, mister," he said. "And you pay me back by playin' up to my squaw."

Glidinghawk met his level glare with one of his own. "Look, Arlie, I didn't ask her to bring any supper out there. It was her idea. And if you don't want me around, I'll ride out right now."

Arlie shook his head and said, "Don't get your

back up. Reckon it ain't your fault Sun Woman keeps forgettin' her place." He waved a hand. "Don't worry about it, Glidinghawk. I'll whomp some respect back into that heathen slut."

Close at his side, Glidinghawk's hand clenched into a fist. Arlie was completely unsuspecting. It would be so easy to slide out the Colt and put a bullet through the bastard's brain.

But then Brass Hand and his braves would riddle him, and that would leave Sun Woman completely defenseless and at the mercy of the Kiowa band.

Glidinghawk knew what would happen to her then.

"Well, get down and come on inside," Arlie said. "We don't need no sentry out at the canyon, not with Brass Hand's boys around. They'll watch out for any strangers."

Glidinghawk hesitated, then swung down from the horse and flipped the reins over the hitch rack. For Sun Woman's sake — as well as for the sake of the mission — he had to play along with Arlie.

As he went inside the cabin with Arlie and Brass Hand, he glanced around the main room and said, "Where's your mother?"

Arlie laughed. "I'm afraid Ma's hidin'. She 'bout went out of her mind when Brass Hand's bunch came ridin' up. And Sun Woman weren't here to calm her down. I swear, I don't understand how that squaw is able to get through to her, but she does. You'd think Ma'd be scared of her, too, the way she feels about Injuns."

187

Brass Hand lifted his jug and let a healthy swallow of the fiery liquor gurgle down his throat. Wiping his mouth, he said, "Injuns not hurt old woman. Arlie's family friends to Kiowa."

"Damn right, Chief," Arlie rejoined, slapping Brass Hand on the back. It was obvious that both men were rapidly getting drunk.

Which could also be said for everyone else in the room with the exception of Glidinghawk. He saw Claude and Dirk passing a jug back and forth. As soon as they finished it, they tossed it aside and reached for another. There were also several Indians sitting around the room, and all of them were drinking.

One of the braves was sitting beside Claude and Dirk, and he was talking animatedly to them. From the markings on his face, Glidinghawk guessed he was some sort of war chief, important but still subordinate to Brass Hand.

Arlie held out his jug to Glidinghawk and said, "Join the party."

Glidinghawk grinned. "Don't mind if I do," he said. He took the jug and tilted it to his lips, working his throat to make it look like he was taking a long swallow. In actuality, though, he kept his lips closed as much as possible and allowed only a little of the whiskey to trickle through. Some of the liquor dribbled down his chin, adding to the illusion.

Dirk stood up and came over to Arlie, clutching at his older brother's arm. "Arlie, come over here!" he said urgently. "You got to hear what this Injun's sayin'." Dirk's eyes shone with excitement.

Arlie allowed Dirk to tug him across the room. Glidinghawk came along, too, wanting to know what was being cooked up.

"Now, what's all this about?" Arlie asked as he joined the small group in the corner.

The Kiowa war chief looked up at him and declared, "We go white man's town, run 'em out! Kill 'em all!" His words were slurred from the whiskey.

"You get it, Arlie?" Claude asked. "They're goin' to raid Truscott!"

Arlie frowned. "Hell, I don't know if that's a good idea or not. We do business with some of the folks there."

"Yeah, but listen to what Dirk and I come up with. Whilst the Injuns are distractin' ever'body, what say we sneak in and get the money out of that there new bank?"

Arlie frowned. "Rob the bank?" he exclaimed.

Glidinghawk held his breath, hoping that Arlie would quickly squash this wild scheme.

"We can get the Injuns to just cause a ruckus and not do much damage," Dirk said quickly. "Claude and me got it all worked out. We give 'em a couple barrels of whiskey to stir the town up, while we hit the bank."

Arlie rubbed at the rough beard stubble on his jaw. "Reckon it could work, all right," he mused.

Glidinghawk leaned forward to get his opinion in.

"That bank is where Davis is going to put the money for his saloon," he pointed out.

"Then it'd be better to hold it up now than later, wouldn't it?" Arlie replied. "Davis's money ain't there yet; he said so hisself."

Glidinghawk suppressed a groan as he saw that his objection had backfired. All he had done was reinforce Arlie's growing opinion that Dirk and Claude had had a good idea.

"I'm still not sure it'd be a good idea," he said, not willing to give up.

"I make the decisions around here," Arlie snapped. He nodded emphatically as he went on, "And I say we do it!"

Glidinghawk shook his head. "I don't want any part of it."

Arlie swung toward him, his hand dropping to the butt of his gun. "If'n you think I'm leavin' you out here by yourself with Sun Woman, you got another think comin', Injun. I been stickin' up for you all along, and you must've got a big head from it." With blinding speed, he drew his pistol and jabbed the muzzle roughly under Glidinghawk's chin. "I'm in charge 'round here, mister, and don't you forget it!"

"All right," Glidinghawk grated. "You made your point, Arlie. You know I'll go along with whatever you say."

Arlie grunted and carefully let down the hammer of the Colt. "Damn right you will." He glanced over at Brass Hand. "C'mere, Chief. We got plans to make." A broad grin split Arlie's ugly face. "We're goin' to rob us a bank."

CHAPTER NINETEEN

Four men rode out of the Brakes and across the plains toward Truscott. Dirk and Claude had not been too happy about Glidinghawk going with them, but Arlie had overruled their objections.

"But how do you know you can trust this redskin, Arlie?" Claude had protested.

"He knows I'll put a slug in his red hide if he crosses us, that's why I trust him."

The two younger brothers had not been able to argue with that.

Benton Moody had come out of his room and slugged down some of the whiskey along with the others. "I can ride," he had insisted. "I want in on this fun."

Arlie shook his head. "Nope. You're healin' up all right, Benton, and we ain't goin' to risk that. You stay here and keep an eye on things for us."

Benton reached down and caressed the Winchester that was lying across his lap. "All right, Arlie. I'll sure do it."

Now the other three Moody brothers and Gerald Glidinghawk were on their way to Truscott, with Brass Hand and his warriors coming along a few minutes behind them.

Arlie, Brass Hand, and the war chief called Busted Tree had worked out the details among themselves while polishing off another couple jugs of whiskey. The Moodys and Glidinghawk would ride into town first and get into position in the alley in back of the bank. Then, a few minutes later, the Kiowas would launch their attack. Arlie had emphasized that Brass Hand and his men were only to make a lot of noise and spook the citizens of Truscott without killing too many people or doing too much damage. While that was happening, Arlie and the others would be able to break into the bank unnoticed.

It was a good plan, Glidinghawk knew, although he thought Arlie was placing too much faith in the Indians' ability to follow orders. Liquored up the way they were, there would probably be a lot more bloodshed than Arlie was counting on.

The Omaha's mind was casting about frantically for a way to ruin this scheme. He had to alert the town to the raid, and somehow, stop the Moodys from robbing the bank.

But Arlie was watching him now, alert for any trouble.

The ride to Truscott seemed to go faster than it should have. When the lights of the town came into view a couple of miles ahead, Glidinghawk still hadn't come up with any way out of this mess. One thing was for sure—before this night was over, his cover identity was going to be useless. Regardless of what happened with the assignment on which Powell's Army had been sent, he had to stop Arlie's plan.

Landrum and Celia were up there in Truscott, not suspecting that bloody-handed trouble was on the way.

It was a peaceful evening in O'Leary's Shamrock Saloon. Landrum and Celia were at the bar, enjoying drinks and conversation with old O'Leary. Several cowboys from the local ranches were lined up at the rail as well, and a few more were playing a friendly game of poker with Garrick. Hughie the barber was sitting at a table in the corner, nursing a beer as he talked to Randolph Watts.

Practically everybody who was anybody in Truscott was in here tonight, Landrum thought as he glanced around the room.

He was feeling pretty good. There had been no problems on his ride back into Truscott from the Moodys' valley. He had arrived just after dark and quickly filled Celia in on what he had discovered. The young redhead had been relieved to find out that Glidinghawk was all right.

"I wish you hadn't had to leave him out there with those cutthroats, though," she'd said.

Landrum had shrugged. "Couldn't be helped right now. The nearest telegraph station is in Seymour. That's about half a day's ride southeast of here. I'll start over there first thing in the morning and get in touch with Amos. Another couple of days and it'll all be over, Celia."

"I hope so." Her own role in this mission had been severely diminished by circumstances, and she didn't like the feeling that things were going along completely out of her control.

Now, the two of them had come to the Shamrock to continue their usual routine. Their cover identities had to be preserved for a little while longer. Landrum had already mentioned casually to O'Leary that he would be riding over to Seymour on business the next day.

Landrum finished his drink and turned away from the bar. "Think I'll sit in on that poker game for a few hands," he said.

"Suit yourself," Celia replied. "I'm a little tired, though. I think I'll walk back home and turn in."

"Want me to go with you?"

Celia smiled. "I think I'll be safe enough in a place like Truscott, Landrum."

He nodded. "You're probably right."

O'Leary spoke up. "'Twould be my honor to walk ye home, Miss Celia."

She smiled at the elderly Irishman. "That's kind of you, Mr. O'Leary, but like I told Landrum, I'm sure I'll be fine."

"Aye. This is a quiet, peaceable town. 'Tis one reason I chose to settle here."

Celia picked up her bag from the bar and pulled her shawl a little tighter around her shoulders. Despite the hot days, the nights were still chilly in this part of the country. She put a hand on Landrum's arm and squeezed lightly. "Good night," she said.

"Night," he returned as he started toward the poker game.

Celia walked out of the saloon, pausing just outside the batwings for a moment to look up at the stars. There was a bright moon tonight, and the stars were brilliant as well. The light they cast bathed the town in a silvery glow.

Celia started down the sidewalk toward the cross street where their rented house was located. Along the way, she had to pass the bank. Her eyes were down, watching the plank boardwalk.

She had no warning of trouble until the rough hand came down brutally on her shoulder.

Glidinghawk and the Moody brothers crouched in the shadows of the alley behind the bank. Arlie and Dirk stood by the back door of the building holding a couple of sledgehammers they had just stolen from the hardware store down the street. They were waiting impatiently for the arrival of the Indians led by Brass Hand. Once the shooting started, it would take only moments to crash in through the heavy door. Several sticks of dynamite

196

were tucked into Dirk's belt; the explosive would be used to deal with the vault door once they were inside.

"Dammit, where are those heathens?" Arlie growled.

Glidinghawk didn't know what was delaying the Kiowas, but he was glad they had not yet shown up. Slowly, he edged away from the other three. His hand stole to the butt of his gun.

There was a good chance he wouldn't be walking away from this, but sometimes the simplest solutions were the best. He would try to get the drop on the three would-be bank robbers. If he was successful, then he could alert the town to the impending Indian raid.

And if the Moodys fought back, the gunfire would do just as good a job of warning the town.

He wished he had gotten a chance to say goodbye to Sun Woman. Landrum would help her, he thought. Even without knowing what had passed between her and Glidinghawk, the Texan would take pity on all four of the squaws and see that they got back to the Nations.

Glidinghawk started to slide his Colt out of its holster.

The sound of heels on the boardwalk came clearly to the ears of the men. Arlie's head jerked around. "Somebody's comin'," he rumbled. "Claude, go see who it is."

Glidinghawk forced himself to relax, not wanting

to start the ball rolling while there was an innocent person so close by. Especially when it was a woman, and unless he was badly mistaken, those were female footsteps he heard.

Claude hurried over to the rear corner of the building and peered toward the street. A second later, he turned around with a grin on his face. "It's that redheaded gal!" he announced in a harsh whisper. "I'm goin' to get her and take her with us!"

Arlie hissed, "Claude! No, dammit!" He was too late, though. Claude had already vanished around the corner of the bank.

The redhead! Glidinghawk knew who Claude had to be talking about. It was Celia, and Claude intended to kidnap her!

Glidinghawk whipped to the corner of the bank, drawing his gun as Arlie yelped, "Glidinghawk! Get back here!" The Omaha reached the corner in time to see Claude lunge out of the darkness and grab Celia by the shoulder. Glidinghawk saw a flash of red hair in the moonlight.

Claude had not counted on getting hold of someone who would fight back. Even as she was gasping in pain and surprise, Celia's hand dove into the bag she carried and came out with the small .38 revolver that was always with her.

Glidinghawk saw the flash of fire from its muzzle, heard the sharp crack of its report. Claude jerked back and howled in pain, clutching at a bullet-shattered shoulder.

Arlie and Dirk dropped their sledgehammers and started toward Glidinghawk.

Glidinghawk spun, the Colt coming out as he did so. "Hold it!" he rapped. "It's all over!"

"You red bastard!" Arlie thundered. "I warned you about double-crossin' me!"

He and Dirk both went for their guns at the same time.

Glidinghawk triggered twice as a war whoop split the night at the other end of town. He saw Dirk stagger backward and drop his gun, but Arlie was untouched. Arlie's gun belched flame and noise, and a slug burned past Glidinghawk's ear.

Glidinghawk threw himself to the side, around the corner of the bank. He was aware of more cries, more gunshots. He thought he heard the crackle of Celia's .38 as she emptied it.

The bitter taste of failure was strong in Glidinghawk's mouth as he stuck the barrel of his gun around the corner and blasted a couple more shots in Arlie's direction. He hadn't been able to warn the town in time, and now Brass Hand and his men would have surprise on their side as they carried out their rampage.

The rumble of running horses filled the air, but over that tumult of noise Glidinghawk was able to hear another horse moving, much closer to him. Arlie must have mounted up, Glidinghawk realized as the hoofbeats clattered down the alley toward him. He dove for the ground as Arlie swept by him, triggering as fast as he could.

The slugs kicked up dust around Glidinghawk, but none of them found their target. Then Arlie was gone, disappearing into the shadows as he fled. That wasn't like him, but with Claude and Dirk both downed, Arlie wasn't going to buck the odds, not even for the money in the bank.

Gunfire swept over the town as the citizens of Truscott hurriedly gathered their wits and began to fight back. Glidinghawk scrambled to his feet, an idea occurring to him. His gun up and ready, he went around the corner into the alley.

Dirk was sprawled motionless on the ground. Glidinghawk kept him covered while he bent over and snagged the dynamite that was tucked in Dirk's belt. There was a huge stain on Dirk's shirt, visible in the moonlight, and his eyes were open and glassy.

Glidinghawk turned away from the corpse and started toward the street, but he had only taken a few steps when a dark shape bulked up in front of him. He barely had time to recognize Claude's face, contorted by hate and pain, before the bigger man smashed into him. Claude's left hand found Glidinghawk's neck and locked on it. His right arm hung limply at his side from the bullet-smashed shoulder.

Staggering, the Omaha caught himself before he fell. Bright lights danced before his eyes, and he

200

didn't know if they were muzzle flashes from the street or simply phantoms of his suddenly oxygen-starved brain.

He forced his muscles to work, bringing up the Colt and ramming it into Claude's belly. The roar of the shot was muffled by the big man's body.

Claude was thrown backward by the horrible impact. He fell, thrashing and screaming as the life bled out of him.

Glidinghawk heaved one breath, then made his shaky legs carry him toward the street. Some still-rational part of his brain realized that his gun was empty, but he wouldn't need it for what he planned to do next. He rammed the weapon back in its holster, then used that hand to dig in his pocket for matches.

There were four sticks of dynamite in his other hand. As he reached the boardwalk, the firing all along the street slacked off abruptly. His eyes darted from side to side, and he spotted Brass Hand's band at the end of the street, where they were evidently gathering for another charge through town.

"Gerald!"

The cry made Glidinghawk jerk his head around. He saw Celia crouched behind a barrel in a nearby doorway. She started to stand up, but Glidinghawk stopped her with a curt gesture.

"Are you all right?" he asked. In the faint glow from a lantern down the street, he could see a dark smear on her cheek, but he couldn't tell if it was blood or dirt.

"I'm fine," she replied. "What about you?"

He scratched a match into life as Brass Hand and Busted Tree both whooped and began galloping down the street, the other warriors riding hard behind them. "I'll be all right in a minute," Glidinghawk said grimly as he lit the fuse on the first stick of dynamite.

"Gerald! No!" Celia cried as he stepped calmly into the street. Sparks flickered brightly in the night air as he threw the first stick of dynamite at the charging Kiowas and then coolly lit the next one.

Glidinghawk felt a bullet tug at his sleeve, but that was the closest any of the shots came. One after the other, he lit the fuses and hurled the explosives into the midst of the suddenly confused Indians. They were trying to turn their ponies and flee when the first stick of dynamite blew up, erupting in flame and death.

Glidinghawk dived to the side, back onto the boardwalk. He buried his face in his arms as three more blasts shook the entire town.

When he looked up again, the Kiowas were in full flight, the townspeople pouring out of the buildings to speed them on their way with a hail of rifle fire.

What was left of Brass Hand and Busted Tree made a bloody mess in the middle of the street.

Glidinghawk felt a strong hand grasping his arm and lifting him. He looked up into Landrum Davis's grinning face. Powdery smoke curled up from the barrel of Landrum's .44. Just behind him, Celia was looking anxiously at Glidinghawk.

"Reckon that was about the craziest stunt I ever did see," Landrum said. "I watched the whole thing from the saloon down there. You all right?"

Glidinghawk nodded. "I don't imagine the Indians will be raiding Truscott again for a while." He jerked his head toward the bunk. "Claude and Dirk Moody are dead back there in the alley. Arlie got away. They were going to rob the bank while those Kiowas provided a distraction."

"Hell of a distraction, all right," Landrum grunted.

"It might have worked if it hadn't been for Celia," Glidinghawk pointed out.

"I . . . I didn't think," the redhead said. "When that man grabbed me, I just went for my gun."

"That was Claude Moody," Glidinghawk told her.

"I reckon Arlie knows now you're not on his side anymore," Landrum said. As the three of them talked, the townspeople began to take stock of the damage caused by the Indians. To Glidinghawk's eye, it didn't look too bad.

Slowly, the Omaha said, "I don't think we can wait for the army now to clean up the Moodys. We're going to have to finish the job ourselves."

Landrum nodded. "We're heading for the

Brakes?"

Glidinghawk thought about Sun Woman and said, "Yes. We're heading for the Brakes."

CHAPTER TWENTY

"I'm going with you," Celia insisted.

Landrum shook his head stubbornly. "No, you're not. It's a long hard ride out there, and Arlie Moody is still on the loose somewhere. Odds are he'll go back to the cabin. I don't want you anywhere around when we're trying to deal with him."

"What are we going to do?" Glidinghawk asked. "We don't have the authority to arrest him."

"No," Landrum said grimly, "we don't. But that won't stop us from wrecking that big still he's got going out there."

"If Arlie's there, he'll try to kill us," Glidinghawk pointed out. His eyes met Landrum's as they stood there on the sidewalk in front of the bank.

"I know," Landrum said flatly.

Randolph Watts came bustling up then, wanting to know what the hell was going on, and Landrum quickly explained about the aborted bank robbery.

Indicating Glidinghawk with a thumb, Landrum went on, "I don't know who this Indian is, but he's the one who saw those men trying to get into the bank. He's the one who ran those renegades off, too."

Landrum spoke hurriedly because already some of

the townspeople were starting to point guns at Glidinghawk. With the raid by Brass Hand's warriors so fresh in their minds, it was easy for them to get spooked by Glidinghawk's buckskins and long dark hair. Better to let them know right away that he was on their side.

Watts calmed folks down after that. He extended his gratitude to Glidinghawk, who accepted as graciously as possible under the circumstances. He and Landrum were both eager to get on the trail out to the Brakes.

Landrum quieted Celia's objections about being left behind by ordering her to catch the morning stage to Seymour and pass along all the information they knew to Amos Powell via telegraph. Although she had agreed, the fiery young redhead didn't like it very much, and she was still complaining when the two men swung up on their horses a few minutes later.

The moon was riding low to the horizon as Landrum and Glidinghawk galloped out of Truscott. They rode hard toward the Brakes, Landrum's rented horse laboring somewhat to keep up with Glidinghawk's mount. The horse was the best one available in Truscott, though, so it would have to do.

It was long after midnight when they reached the beginning of the narrow canyon that led into the Moodys' valley. They brought their horses to a halt and dismounted.

"We'd better go the rest of the way on foot," Glidinghawk said in low-pitched tones. "Arlie could be waiting up there at that lookout post."

"You think he'll be expecting you?" Landrum asked.

"I'll be surprised if he's not. He knows I turned on them back there in town." Glidinghawk said nothing about Arlie's suspicion that there was something between Sun Woman and the Omaha. That would be one more reason Arlie might expect Glidinghawk to return to the valley.

They would have to kill Arlie and Benton in order to destroy the still. Glidinghawk felt sure of that. Maybe it was taking the law into their own hands— he didn't want to think about that. Circumstances had brought them to this.

Circumstances—and the evil brought into the world by Arlie Moody.

They tied their horses to a couple of the scrub mesquite that dotted the area and then catfooted their way into the canyon. The moon was low enough now that it cast no light into the steep-sided passage. The two men were moving slowly and carefully through almost total darkness, their guns out and ready.

Glidinghawk took the lead and trailed one hand along the wall of the canyon to keep himself oriented. Landrum followed closely behind him. Neither man spoke, but they could hear each other's breathing in the thick shadows.

Glidinghawk paused when he judged that they

were close to the sentry post. His keen ears strained for any sound that might indicate Arlie was waiting for them — heavy breathing, the clink of metal against rock, anything like that.

There was nothing, no sound.

After five long minutes, Glidinghawk reached behind him to touch Landrum's shoulder and indicate they would go on.

They reached the end of the canyon and paused on the edge of the valley. The high bluffs that surrounded the area on three sides cast long shadows that left most of the valley floor in darkness. The cabin itself was still in the edge of moonlight, about half a mile away. Glidinghawk and Landrum started toward it, moving more quickly now.

Smoke drifted up from the chimney of the smaller building where the still was located. The fire was going there under the boiler. Arlie was continuing to make whiskey.

Landrum and Glidinghawk dropped into a crouch behind some brush when they were fifty yards away from the cabin. "What now?" Landrum hissed. "You know this setup better than I do."

"Benton's probably inside the cabin with Ma and a couple of the squaws. Arlie could be anywhere. He may not even be here, Landrum."

"Where else would he go?"

Glidinghawk didn't have an answer for that. "I'll take the cabin," he said. "You head for the still. If you run up against either of the brothers, shoot fast, because they won't be giving you a second chance."

"I know that," Landrum agreed grimly.

They started forward, Glidinghawk heading straight for the main cabin, Landrum veering toward the other building. Glidinghawk lost sight of his companion as he reached the porch of the cabin.

Pausing momentarily, Glidinghawk listened. A frown etched his face at what he heard coming from inside the building.

Someone was singing.

It was a high, reedy female voice that was warbling through an off-key rendition of a hymn. Ma Moody, Glidinghawk decided. It sounded as if she was inside the big main room.

He had traded his boots for moccasins before entering the canyon, and his steps now made no noise as he climbed onto the porch. The butt of the Colt gripped tightly in his hand, he went to the partially open doorway. A faint light, as if from a single candle, came through it.

Glidinghawk pushed the door open and stepped through, eyes darting from side to side, the barrel of the gun tracking across the room.

Ma Moody sat in an old rocking chair by the cold fireplace. She was still singing as Glidinghawk came into the room, but she broke off the hymn and jerked up the shotgun that had been resting in her lap.

Glidinghawk's instincts had the Colt lined on her frail form and his finger pressing on the trigger before he knew what was happening. At the last instant, he hesitated, not wanting to kill the old woman.

The door to the kitchen burst open, and Benton Moody lunged through it, rifle in hand. He screamed, "Redskin bastard!" as the Winchester blasted. The crack of the rifle was all but lost in the roar of the shotgun.

Glidinghawk dropped to the floor as the weapons thundered. Benton's bullet was a clean miss, and he dodged most of the buckshot as well, since the charge hadn't had time to spread much. Several of the lead pellets stabbed fiery pain into his leg, though.

As he landed hard on his belly, he jerked the Colt toward Benton and triggered twice. The slugs caught Benton in the chest, knocking him back against the wall. He hung there for a moment, the rifle falling from his suddenly nerveless hands, and then pitched forward on his face, dead when he hit the floor.

Glidinghawk rolled, dragging his wounded leg behind him, and brought the pistol to bear on Ma Moody again. She had fired both barrels at once this time, and as she rose from the rocking chair, she flung the empty weapon at Glidinghawk. He threw up an arm to block it. The barrel of the shotgun cracked painfully across his forearm.

He rose from the floor, keeping Ma covered. The old woman's watery eyes went to the sprawled body of her son, then back to Glidinghawk's bleak face. She raised her clawlike hands and covered her lined features. A shriek of pure horror tore from her

210

throat.

Then her head dropped back and she slumped to the floor in a dead faint, overcome by her insane fear of Indians.

Glidinghawk closed his eyes for a moment and took a deep breath.

Then he strode over to the kitchen door and kicked it open.

Three squaws were huddling in a corner of the room, eyes wide with terror. None of them was Sun Woman, he saw immediately.

"You're safe," he told them. "I won't hurt you. Benton's dead, and Ma's passed out. If I were you, I'd tie her up so that she can't get into any more trouble. Can you do that?"

He wasn't sure how much they would understood in their fear, but one of them slowly nodded.

"Now, where's Sun Woman?" he asked.

The sudden crackle of gunfire from the other building was the only answer he got.

If she wasn't here, she had to be out there.

Glidinghawk bulled through the back door of the cabin and headed for the other building at a dead run. He didn't even notice the pain of his wounded leg until it gave on him. He stumbled, catching his balance, and then before he could run any further, the door of the other building crashed open.

Glidinghawk saw two figures struggling desperately as they half fell through the doorway. They were silhouetted by the leaping flames of the fire underneath the boiler.

The fighting men lost their balance and fell, rolling over and over in the red dust of the hard ground. First Arlie was on top, then Landrum. The firelight cast a harsh red glare over their faces.

Glidinghawk stood several yards away, his gun out but unable to fire. There was too much of a chance of hitting Landrum. A knife flashed in Arlie's hand.

Landrum's booted foot lashed out, connecting with Arlie's wrist with a sharp crack. The knife sailed away into the darkness. But before Landrum could seize the advantage, Arlie brought his knee up in a savage thrust into the Texan's groin. Landrum doubled over in pain.

Arlie rolled away from him, surging onto his feet. He was still wearing the thick buffalo coat, and his hand darted beneath it to come out with another pistol.

"Arlie!" Glidinghawk yelled.

Arlie froze, his gun pointed at Landrum's head. He looked up, across Landrum's body, and saw Glidinghawk. A grin spread across Arlie's beard-stubbled face as he saw the Omaha's gun lined up on him.

"Looks like we got a standoff, Injun," Arlie called. "Reckon you can drop me, all right, but not in time to keep me from blastin' your friend's brains right out'n his head!"

"Forget it, Arlie, it's over," Glidinghawk said. "All your brothers are dead, and the army knows about this place." That was stretching the truth a little, but

Arlie wouldn't know that. "You might as well give up. At least you'll still be alive."

"Yeah—until I get hung! No thanks, redskin." Arlie's grin widened. "Reckon instead of shootin' your friend, though—I'll kill you!"

He yanked the muzzle of the gun toward Glidinghawk, crouching as he did so.

A lithe shape in buckskins flew out of the building, darting in front of Arlie just as he jerked the trigger.

"Sun Woman!" Glidinghawk screamed.

The crash of Arlie's gun came plainly to his ears, but he couldn't see the spout of flame from the muzzle. Sun Woman's body blocked that. She spun away, clutching at her middle and staggering.

"Noooo!" Glidinghawk cried as he triggered the gun in his hand.

The bullets smashed into Arlie Moody, driving him backward in a macabre dance of death. Glidinghawk kept pulling the trigger even after Arlie's body had spilled limply to the ground.

Then slowly, Glidinghawk became aware that the hammer was falling on empty chambers. He blinked and lowered the gun.

Landrum Davis pulled himself onto his feet, shaking his head. Still bent over slightly from the pain of Arlie's blow, he went over to the body of the whiskey smuggler and prodded it with a toe.

Arlie was dead, all right, his chest a bloody ruin.

Glidinghawk went to Sun Woman's side and knelt there, gently rolling her onto her back. Her eyes

213

were closed, but they opened as he hovered over her.

"G-Glidinghawk," she whispered.

"Sun Woman," he said, a hard fist clutching his heart and squeezing the soul from him.

"Could not . . . let Arlie . . . hurt Glidinghawk," Sun Woman gasped.

He swallowed. "We were going to leave here together."

"No . . . no place for us to go . . . no place for Sun Woman . . . better . . . this way . . ."

After that, there was no sound for long moment except the crackling of the fire underneath the boiler. Glidinghawk stared dry-eyed at her face as the features smoothed over in death.

He was not a man who cried. Not now.

Perhaps someday.

Landrum's hand fell on Glidinghawk's shoulder. "Don't know who she was, Gerald," he said softly, "but I'm sorry."

"She was a good woman," Glidinghawk said as he straightened. "A better woman than even she knew."

Landrum inclined his head toward the still. "We'd better put out that fire. It's burning a little high."

Glidinghawk turned his bleak eyes toward the building. He shook his head. "No," he said simply.

There was a stack of short lengths of firewood by the door of the building. Glidinghawk went to it and picked up several of the pieces of wood. He tossed them through the doorway, into the blaze underneath the boiler. The flames died down for a moment, then

214

leaped up higher than ever.

Landrum clutched his arm. "Dammit, there's a bunch of barrels of whiskey stored in there. You know what'll happen if that boiler gets too hot?"

Glidinghawk just looked at him, then threw more wood on the fire. He knew, all right, and Landrum realized that he knew.

Slowly, Landrum nodded.

The blaze grew as Glidinghawk gently lifted Sun Woman's body and carried her into the building. He placed her close to the door, stripping off his buckskin shirt and folding it to pillow her head. The heat from the fire beat against his bare skin, but he hardly felt it.

"Come on," Landrum said, his tone urgent. "That boiler can't last much longer."

Glidinghawk nodded and took one last look at Sun Woman's face. She might have almost been sleeping. . . .

They got the squaws and Ma Moody out of the main cabin. Ma's hands were tied, as Glidinghawk had suggested. She had regained consciousness, and she seemed to have lost her fear. Her eyes were empty now, and she was meekly cooperative as Landrum herded her along.

Glidinghawk caught four horses from the corral and let the others run free. He led the horses while Landrum kept Ma and the squaws walking toward the canyon. The buckshot wounds in Glidinghawk's leg were just a dull ache now, a pain he could easily ignore.

The moon was gone now, but the night sky was suddenly lit up. The earth shook, and the blast from the still as the boiler exploded assaulted their ears. That was just the beginning, though.

The stored whiskey went up with a tremendous roar, sending a column of flame high into the air. The other cabin caught fire as well and burned rapidly.

Landrum and the others looked back at the inferno—all but Glidinghawk.

There was nothing there for him to see, no reason for him to turn around.

All he could do now was look forward. . . .

CHAPTER TWENTY-ONE

Preston Kirkwood Fox stepped out onto the porch of the Indian agent's office at Fort Supply, Indian Territory. There was a cigar in his mouth and a worried look on his young face. Nearly two weeks had passed since Glidinghawk had disappeared from the stockade. In that time, Fox had not heard a word from either the Omaha or Landrum and Celia.

What the devil had happened to them? Had their mission failed?

Was he the only member of Powell's Army left alive?

There was a warm breeze this morning. It was going to be a lovely late spring day. Fox paid little attention to the beauties of nature. He had been thinking for several days that he was going to have to get in touch with Colonel Amos Powell and request new orders to deal with this situation. Now he had come to a decision.

He was going to the telegraph station at the fort's headquarters and send a carefully coded telegram to Powell.

As Fox started across the parade ground with renewed vigor in his step, Sergeant Bradley Foster came through the door of the sutler's store and hailed him. "Mornin', Mr. Follett," the supply sergeant said as he came down the stairs to fall in step beside Fox. "How are you?"

"Why, I'm fine," Fox replied. Foster had been rather friendly with him ever since Glidinghawk's escape.

"Any word on that buck that ran away?" Foster asked.

Fox shook his head. "I'm afraid not. I don't think we'll ever see him again, to tell you the truth."

Fox frowned in thought as he walked. Foster had been quite curious about Glidinghawk, and Fox was beginning to wonder why.

Maybe, Fox thought, Foster had had something to do with the Omaha's escape on that stormy night. . . .

Several men rode through the fort's gate and trotted their horses over to the commanding officer's office. Fox studied them curiously. They wore the uniforms of officers, two majors and a lieutenant. He didn't recall seeing them around Fort Supply before.

Bradley Foster saw the newcomers, too. "Fresh meat," he said, chuckling. "I'd heard we were going to get some new officers. Well, the noncoms will get them straightened out soon enough."

Fox bit back the sharp retort he wanted to make. Foster's arrogant attitude toward commissioned officers was common among the lower ranks, but that didn't excuse it. Maybe he could find some subtle

218

way to pass along the sergeant's insubordination to Colonel Selmon.

As the new officers swung down from their mounts, one of the majors glanced over at Fox. There was something familiar about him. . . .

"Preston!" the major called loudly. "Preston Fox! How are you, old boy?"

Fox suddenly felt as if the bottom of his stomach had dropped out. He recognized the major as one of his classmates from West Point, an insufferably studious type named . . . Hackett, that was it. Not only had he graduated ahead of Fox, but he had had the bad habit of often being right.

Fox tried desperately to regain his wits even as Major Hackett strode forward and grasped his hand, pumping it up and down. Finally, Fox managed to say, "I-I'm sorry, sir, but I don't believe I know you."

"Sure you do," the major insisted. "I'm Curt Hackett. We were at West Point together." He frowned. "What are you doing out of uniform, Lieutenant? Or have you been promoted, too?"

Fox shook his head. "I'm truly sorry, but you're mistaken, Major. My name is Preston Follett. I'm the Indian agent assigned here."

Even to his own ears, the claim rang false. He glanced over and saw Foster studying him intently.

"I'm sorry, Major, but I have to go," Fox said hurriedly. He walked quickly away, his intention to send a telegram to Amos Powell completely forgotten.

Behind him, Major Hackett shrugged. Fox heard

him say, "He always was a strange one, that Fox. Well, come on, men, let's report to Colonel Selmon and deliver that dispatch to him."

Fox went back to his office and settled down behind his desk, pulling a handkerchief from his pocket to mop the sweat from his face. What devilishly bad luck! Ever since he had gone undercover with Powell's Army, he had worried that someday he would run into someone who would recognize him. Now it had happened.

What would be the result? Foster had been looking awfully suspiciously at him. If the supply sergeant was indeed involved in the case, would this misfortune tip him off that Fox was an investigator?

There was nothing he could do now except wait to see what happened.

He took a small pistol from a drawer in the desk and checked to make sure it was loaded.

Fox didn't have to wait long. A few minutes later, Bradley Foster opened the door of the office and came in. Fox sat up straighter and tried to make his voice strong as he asked, "What can I do for you, Sergeant?"

Foster pulled a chair over, reversed it, and straddled it. He pushed his campaign hat to the back of his head. "Sure was strange the way that new major thought you were somebody else, wasn't it?" he said without preamble.

"He made a mistake," Fox declared. "It happens to everybody. No harm done."

"Maybe not. But it sure starts a fella wonderin'. Now me, I wonder why somebody who's really in the army would pretend that he's not. Seems like a fella who did that would have something to hide." Foster slid his service revolver from its holster and leaned it on the back of the chair, the muzzle negligently turned toward Fox. "How about you, Mr. Follet—or is it Lieutenant Fox? What have you got to hide?"

Fox paled. His own gun was resting in the open drawer, only inches from his fingers, but Foster had the drop on him.

"You must be mad!" Fox exclaimed. "What do you hope to accomplish by this, Foster?"

"I just want to know who you are," Foster said grimly.

"You know quite well, I'm an Indian agent—"

"I don't think so," Foster cut in. "I think you came here looking for whoever's helping smuggle whiskey into the Nations from Texas. Am I right?"

Fox was unable to keep the surprise off his face. Foster had everything figured out. Fox's bluff had not fooled him for an instant.

"You can't get away with this!" Fox blustered. "I'm onto you now, Foster. You might as well surrender. What can you do? You can't just murder me right here in the middle of the fort!" His voice grew stronger as he went on.

"No, but the two of us can take a ride out onto the reservation to see how them poor heathens are doing." Foster grinned, but it was an ugly expression.

221

"You see, Fox or whatever your name is, I ain't got a whole lot to lose."

"I . . . I . . ."

Foster cocked an eyebrow. "Why don't you take a chance? Live a little longer, maybe something good will happen. Or I can just shoot you right here and try to fight my way out of here. I tell you this much, I ain't goin' to hang, and I ain't goin' to spend the next thirty years in the stockade. I'd rather take a bullet right now."

There was no doubting Foster's sincerity. Sweat rolled down Fox's brow, and his fingers shook as he placed his hands on top of his desk. He started to stand up. "I . . . I suppose we could take that ride," he quavered.

"Good idea," Foster said. He scraped his chair back.

There were heavy footsteps on the porch outside the office. Fox glanced up, and through the window he saw not only Major Hackett but also Colonel Selmon.

And both of them had their pistols in their hands.

Foster's head swiveled, and he saw the same thing Fox did. The sergeant's face twisted in rage and frustration, and he jerked his pistol toward the window.

Fox heard it roar as he dove for the floor behind the desk.

Then he heard the shattering of glass as more gunshots rang out. Foster grunted as lead thudded into his body. He staggered back against the desk, mortally wounded by Selmon and Hackett, his gun slipping from his fingers. He went to his knees, then fell forward.

His head twisted as he hit the floor, and Fox found himself staring into Foster's dead eyes.

Selmon and Hackett crashed in through the door of the office. The colonel bent over Foster's body while Hackett hurried around the desk to help Fox to his feet. "You all right, Preston?" he asked.

"Yes," Fox said. "But please—I'm Preston Follett, understand?"

Hackett shrugged. "Whatever you say, Mr. Follett," he replied in low tones. "I suppose you've got a good reason."

Selmon swung to face Fox. "What happened here?"

Fox gestured at the dead sergeant, thinking frantically as he tried to come up with a believable answer. "He—he tried to rob me. He was running away for some reason—"

"He was running away because he must have figured out somehow that I was going to arrest him," Selmon said heavily. "This is army business, Follett, but I suppose you have a right to know. Major Hackett here just delivered a dispatch from the adjutant general's office advising me that Sergeant Foster here was part of a scheme to smuggle illegal whiskey into Indian Territory."

"The . . . the adjutant general's office?"

"Yes. Colonel Amos Powell, specifically." Selmon grunted. "I'm not sure how he knew about Foster, but the military has a way of finding these things out. From Foster's reaction, I'd say that Colonel Powell's information was correct."

Fox nodded, relief flooding through him. Not only had he been rescued from Foster in the nick of time, but it looked as if Landrum and Celia and Glidinghawk were probably all right. They had to be the ones who had supplied the information to Colonel Powell.

That meant he would be leaving soon. "Preston Follett" would be reassigned to some other agency, thence to disappear. New missions, new cover identities, would be waiting.

The military had a way of finding things out, all right — a weapon known only to a few — Powell's Army.